CERVANTES
DON QUIXOTE

being a faithful translation and adaptation
by Magda Bogin
of the first part of Cervantes's original classic
published in 1605
masterfully illustrated by Manuel Boix

STEWART, TABORI & CHANG   NEW YORK

Text copyright ©1991 Magda Bogin
Illustrations copyright ©1991 Manuel Boix

Published in 1991 by
Stewart, Tabori & Chang, Inc.
575 Broadway, New York, New York 10012

Library of Congress Cataloging-in-Publication Data

Bogin, Magda.
Cervantes Don Quixote:
being a faithful translation and adaptation
of the first part of Cervantes's original classic
published in 1605 / by Magda Bogin; masterfully
illustrated by Manuel Boix.
p. cm.
ISBN 1-55670-201-9
I. Boix, Manuel. II. Cervantes Saavedra, Miguel de, 1547-1616.
Don Quixote. III. Title.
PQ6329.A3   1991   91-13902
863'.3 – dc20   CIP

Distributed in the U.S. by Workman Publishing,
708 Broadway, New York, New York 10003
Distributed in Canada by Canadian Manda Group,
P.O. Box 920 Station U, Toronto, Ontario M8Z 5P9
Distributed in all other territories by
Little, Brown and Company, International Division,
34 Beacon Street, Boston, Massachusetts 02108

Printed in Italy
10 9 8 7 6 5 4 3 2 1

LIST OF ILLUSTRATIONS

PART ONE

Once upon a time, in a village of La Mancha, there lived a certain gentleman whose lance was always at the ready. He also kept an ancient shield, a scrawny horse, and a greyhound for the chase. A bowl of stew and a plate of hash most weeknights, groans and bones on Saturdays, lentil soup on Fridays, and a tender pigeon every Sunday took up three-quarters of this good man's income. The rest he spent on a costume of the best brocade, with velvet breeches and matching shoes for feast days, and a suit of homespun to wear during the week. His household consisted of a housekeeper well past the age of forty, a niece still under twenty, and a jack-of-all-trades who did everything from saddling the horse to trimming hedges.

This nobleman, who was nearing fifty, was tough of stock, taut of frame, and gaunt of face, and he loved nothing more than rising early and riding to the hunt. Some say his name was Quijada; others call him Quesada or Quixana. But that has little bearing on our tale. Our only task is not to stray one iota from the truth.

It should be said that our gentleman's free time—which was practically the whole year round—was devoted to reading tales of knights and ladies, in which he became so engrossed that he very nearly forgot about his hunting and the maintenance of his estate. In fact, so carried away did he become with these tales of chivalry, as they are called, that he sold some of his finest planting fields to keep himself supplied with books. He spent his nights reading until daybreak, and his days reading until nightfall; and before long, what with too little sleep and too much reading, his brain dried up like a raisin and he lost his mind.

His head swam with fantastic images from all the books he had read—bewitchings and spells, hangings and duels, contests and quarrels, romances and dances and every kind of unimaginable occurrence; and these dreamlike things became so real to him that he believed there was no truer story in the world.

In fact, with his wits gone, he soon fell prey to the strangest thought that ever crossed a madman's mind. Namely, that for his personal honor and the greater glory of his country, he should become a wandering knight like those he read about, and ride forth on horseback, fully armed, to seek his fortune, risking body and soul in good deeds that would win him everlasting fame.

The first thing he did was dust off a rusty suit of armor that had belonged to his ancestors. Only after he had polished it as best he could and stood it on its feet did he realize there was something missing: the helmet had no visor. Never one to be discouraged, he cut some cardboard into a half-visor and attached it to the helmet. Then, to see if it was strong enough, he took out his sword and struck it twice; the first blow destroyed in an instant what it had taken him a week to make. He was taken aback at the ease with which he had demolished his creation, but quickly started over, this time shaping it around a metal frame. Reluctant to test his luck a second time, and convinced that the new visor would withstand all challenges, he pronounced his handiwork a perfect helmet perfectly constructed.

Then he went to see his horse. He spent four days trying to invent a name for it, believing (so he told himself) that the horse of such a famous knight should have a famous name, a name, what's more, that would suggest not only what the animal had been before, but what it had become now that it belonged to a knight errant. Finally, after toying with this name and that, crossing one out and putting one in, changing one this way and changing one that, he hit upon Rocinante, from *rocin* (horse) and *antes* (before). Not only was this name melodious and lofty, it conveyed exactly what his mount had been when it was just an ordinary horse, before it was what it was now, when it came before all other horses in the world.

Now it was his own turn. He spent a whole week lost in thought, and when he was done he was ready to be called Don Quixote. But then he remembered brave Amadis, his hero from the age of chivalry, who had taken the name of his birthplace and become Amadis of Gaul. Our good gentleman decided to do the same, becoming Don Quixote de la Mancha, which he hoped would bring honor to his homeland and renown to his descendants.

His armor restored, his helmet visored, and both his horse and himself duly renamed, there remained only one important task: he had to find a lady. For a knight without a lady is like a tree without leaves or a body without a soul. After all, he told himself, if I come across some giant, and if, as so often happens with knights errant, I slay him with a single stroke and slice him in two, or if I conquer him in battle and take him captive, wouldn't it be nice to have a lady before whom he can fall to his knees and beg for mercy?

As luck would have it, in a town not far from his, there lived a lovely farm girl by the name of Aldonza Lorenzo, who had once stolen his heart. He liked the idea of making her the lady of his thoughts. And as he sought a name not too different from her own but one that would suggest and befit a princess and great lady, he settled on Dulcinea del Toboso, El Toboso being the town where she was born. This name was both musical and strange, it seemed to him, and as full of meaning as all the others he had given himself and his possessions.

Now that everything had been arranged, Don Quixote was eager to leave home without delay. After all, with every passing hour he was depriving the world of his good deeds: the crooks he would catch, the debts he would pay, the wrongs he would right, the lives he would save. So, one hot summer morning while it was still dark out, he put on his armor, drew his makeshift visor down over his forehead, climbed onto Rocinante, and without a whisper or a word to anyone, slipped through an opening in the far wall of his courtyard, his heart brimming with pride at how easy it had been to make his vision a reality.

But as the broad fields opened up before him, he was gripped by a terrifying thought: he had never sworn the oath of knighthood, which meant he had no business riding to anybody's rescue. This nearly caused him to turn back, but fortunately his madness overcame what his mind couldn't. Remembering his beloved tales of chivalry, he decided to be dubbed a knight by the first man to cross his path, whereupon he breathed a great sigh of relief and resumed his journey, letting Rocinante lead the way.

"Happy the age," our adventurer said aloud as they trotted along, "and happy the day, when my glorious deeds will be engraved in bronze and carved in marble, to be known around the world for all eternity. And you," he went on, "who will one day tell my tale, whoever you may be, see that you pay due respect to Rocinante, companion of my every step." That wasn't all. "Sweet Dulcinea," he continued, "princess of my heart! Prithee, lady, think kindly on thy humble servant, who has toiled far from Thy Worship ever since thee banished me with thy cruel words."

With this and similar nonsense he rattled on, traveling so slowly in the midday sun that his brains would have melted clear away—if he had any left.

By evening both horse and rider were thoroughly exhausted. As Don Quixote scanned the horizon for a place to spend the night, he spied an inn not far ahead. But when they neared the gates, it seemed more like a castle with four shimmering towers, a drawbridge, and a moat. While he was admiring this view, a swineherd looking for a wayward pig ran down the road, blowing on a special horn. Convinced the lord of the castle had sent a royal trumpeter to herald his arrival, Don Quixote rode up to the doorway, where two beautiful princesses (actually two coarse young girls) were taking the evening air. They turned in terror when they saw him, but he lifted his cardboard visor, revealing his dry, dusty face, and addressed them as gently as he could.

"Flee not, sweet majesties, for by the rule of chivalry which I profess, no harm shall come to anyone, least of all such distinguished maidens as thyselves."

The girls could hardly keep from laughing at the stranger's quaint appearance and even quainter way of speaking.

At this point the innkeeper, a placid, roly-poly man, appeared in the doorway. He too would have burst out laughing if not for the thought that great harm could come to him from all that mismatched armor.

The innkeeper held Rocinante's stirrups while Don Quixote dismounted, so faint with hunger that he almost fell straight to the ground.

The two young girls brought him a sorry piece of fish with some bread as dark and dingy as his armor, and set up a table in the doorway to take advantage of the cool night air. Don

Quixote could barely eat through his helmet (he had fastened it with bright green ribbons that he refused to let them cut) and would have been unable to drink had not the innkeeper threaded a straw through the visor, which allowed him to empty a carafe of wine directly into his guest's mouth.

Thus wined and dined, Don Quixote fell to his knees, refusing to rise until his host granted him a special favor which, he promised, would benefit not just himself but the entire human race.

"Tonight, my lord," said Don Quixote, "if you agree, I will keep vigil in your castle, and tomorrow, thanks to Your Grace, I will ride out across the world to help the needy and lift up the fallen, as befits a true knight errant."

The innkeeper, who already suspected that his guest was mad, decided to play along with this request. He too, he said, had once been a knight errant. In his day he had crisscrossed Spain from north to south, righting enough wrongs and wronging enough of his fellow citizens to make a name for himself in every court of law from Toledo to Seville.

He would be more than happy to administer the oath of knighthood. If Don Quixote agreed, the ceremony would take place the following morning, and he would become a knight— such a knight, the innkeeper assured him, that there would be no knight quite like him in the whole wide world.

Don Quixote promised to do just as he was told. With no further ado, he spread his armor on a trough, placed his shield over his arm, thrust his lance into the air, and began to pace up and down the courtyard under the full moon. The innkeeper went off to tell his other guests about the madman who wanted to be dubbed a knight, and before long a crowd had gathered in the shadows to watch his strange performance.

Meanwhile, a muleteer who was staying at the inn went out to water his mules. "Stand back, rash knight," roared Don Quixote as the man approached the trough, "and keep your

hands off the armor of the bravest knight ever to wield a sword, lest you pay for your folly with your life!"

Unperturbed, the muleteer swept the armor from the trough. Don Quixote raised his eyes to Heaven. "Assist me, lady," he implored, as if addressing his lady Dulcinea, "in this first adventure of my life as a knight errant." Following this imprecation, he dropped his shield, gripped his lance with both his hands, and dealt the muleteer a fierce blow to the head that knocked him cold.

Now a second muleteer appeared. Unaware of what had happened to the first (who lay spread as flat as paper on the ground), he too approached the trough, intending to water his mules. Without a word of warning, Don Quixote raised his lance over his head and cleft the poor man's skull in half. When the friends of the two men saw what had happened, a hail of stones immediately followed. But Don Quixote shouted so loud that they withdrew in fright, and he resumed his vigil, pacing back and forth before his armor.

By this point, the innkeeper had had enough. Hoping

to avoid further misfortunes, he apologized for the rudeness of the other guests and proclaimed that by his valor and the fact that four hours had passed, Don Quixote had fully satisfied the requirements of knighthood. With the two maidens in attendance, he began to read from the ledger in which he kept his household accounts, while a young boy held aloft a half-burned candle. Midway through, he grabbed Don Quixote's sword and struck him sharply on the neck, then on the shoulder, continuing to read in a pious voice as if he were saying his devotions.

"May God make Your Worship a fortunate knight and grant you success in all your endeavors," one of the young girls proclaimed, and with that the ceremony was complete.

Don Quixote could hardly contain his excitement. He saddled Rocinante and, in language too flowery to reproduce, thanked the innkeeper for knighting him. The innkeeper, as eager to be rid of him as Don Quixote was to leave, replied in equally ridiculous terms and, without charging him for the night's stay, wished him Godspeed on his journey.

It was almost daybreak when Don Quixote rode out onto the open road, so happy, so buoyant, and so pleased at finally being dubbed a knight that his joy almost split his horse's girths. But he decided to turn back toward his village where, he thought, he would stock up on food and set out again with a loyal neighbor as his squire. As if reading his mind, Rocinante flew along so swiftly that his hooves scarcely touched the ground.

They had gone only a short way when he saw six men with parasols not far ahead, silk traders from Toledo as he later learned, who were traveling to Murcia, accompanied by four servants on horseback and three muleteers on foot. He could hardly believe his luck, for it was a scene straight from his favorite books. He drew himself up in his saddle, thrust his boots into his stirrups, gripped his lance with a firm hand, and raised his shield to his chest.

"Halt!" he thundered as soon as these other knights rode into view (for knights they assuredly must be). "And ride no more until you declare my lady Dulcinea del Toboso, empress of La Mancha, the most beautiful maid in all the world!" The merchants reined in their horses and stared at the strange figure in the middle of the road, whose speech and dress told them he was mad.

"Good knight," one of them began, more for his own amusement than for anything else, "we do not know the lady of whom you speak. However, if she is as lovely as you say, bring her here so we may gaze on her with our own eyes, and we shall gladly swear to what you ask."

"If you could see her," roared Don Quixote, "what would be the value of your oath? Don't you understand? The point is to believe in her beauty without setting eyes on her. Otherwise we are at war, O base and vile men!"

"Good knight," replied the merchant, "don't force us to proclaim a truth we haven't seen with our own eyes or heard with our own ears. In the name of my fellow princes, at least show us a portrait of your lady, be it ever so small as a grain of wheat, so that we may swear in all good faith. Even if she is cross-eyed or hunchbacked, once we have seen her we will gladly say whatever you like."

"Dog!" cried Don Quixote. "Her eyes are as beautiful as amber, her back as straight as the straightest poplar in all Spain." With that he thrust his lance at the insolent trader and would have left him in a dismal state indeed had Rocinante not tripped and stumbled at that very moment, sending Don Quixote sprawling across the field. From where, weighed down by his lance, his shield, his spurs, his helmet, and his ancient armor, he was unable to move—a fact which did not, however, immobilize his tongue.

"Flee not, vile cowards! For by no fault of mine do I lie prostrate!"

One of the young muleteers had heard enough. He grabbed Don Quixote's lance, snapped it in half, and proceeded to

beat him with the pieces until the merchants begged him to relent. When his arm finally tired, they resumed their journey, telling of their strange adventure everywhere they stopped along the way.

Once they were gone, Don Quixote tried to move again, but it was no use; hard as it had been before, it was even harder now that he'd been beaten black-and-blue. There was nothing for it but to resort to his usual cure, which was to lose himself in his favorite tales. As luck would have it, while he lay there telling himself the story of the duke of Mantua, which is known to every man, woman, and child, a neighbor of his happened up the road on his way back from the mill. When the peasant heard the gibberish the wounded man was muttering under his breath, he bent down to see who it was and what was wrong. As soon as he raised Don Quixote's visor and wiped the dust from his face, he immediately recognized his neighbor.

"Master Quijana!" he exclaimed. "Who has done you such terrible harm?"

But Don Quixote chattered on, telling one tale after another and addressing his neighbor by every name under the sun.

The good man piled Don Quixote's weapons across Rocinante's back, lifted him up onto his own mount, and, leading both horses by the reins, set off in the direction of their village, lost in thought.

"Listen to me," he interrupted at last, "I am not the duke of Mantua or Rodrigo de Narvaez but your friend and neighbor Pedro Alonso. And you, good sir, are none other than Señor Quijana."

"I know who I am," said Don Quixote, "and I know that I can be any of the characters I have just named, for my exploits are far greater than all the deeds they have done combined."

By the time they reached the village it was growing dark, but Don Quixote's neighbor decided to wait until nightfall so no one would see his friend in such a pitiful state. They found Don Quixote's house in an uproar. The village priest and barber were in the kitchen with his housekeeper and niece, who were frantic with worry since they had seen neither hide nor hair of him for three whole days.

"A pox on all those books of chivalry that filled his head with foolishness!" the housekeeper exclaimed.

"If only I had thought to tell you about my uncle's madness," the niece chimed in, "you could have burned those cursed books, which deserve to perish in the flames like any ordinary sinner."

"As a matter of fact," the priest replied, "I hereby promise to do just that tomorrow morning. We don't want some other soul to read them and do what your dear uncle has assuredly done."

The neighbor, who was waiting outside with Don Quixote, decided it was time to announce their arrival. Everyone inside the house came running, but Don Quixote stopped them in their tracks. "Halt!" he shouted, "I am grievously wounded. Take me to my bed!" They carried him upstairs, laid him gently in his bed, and examined him from head to toe. When they failed to find a single wound, Don Quixote explained that he had fallen from his horse while fighting off ten fire-breathing giants, the most fearsome anywhere on earth, and that he was merely bruised.

They plied him with questions, but he refused to answer, asking only for food and sleep. The peasant told the priest how he had found him lying in the middle of a field, and recounted all the claptrap Don Quixote had told him as they rode back to the village. This only made the priest more eager to do what he would do the following day, when he and the barber returned to see their good friend Don Quixote...

...Who was sound asleep and snoring when they arrived. The priest and the barber tiptoed up to his library with his niece leading the way. When she turned the key in the door they found more than a hundred books, some thick, some thin, and all handsomely bound.

The priest asked the barber to hand him the volumes one by one, in case there were any that deserved to be spared.

"Not the prayer of a chance," the niece remarked. "They're each as guilty as the next. You might as well just throw them from the window and burn them where they land—or, if you prefer, we can build a bonfire in back, where the smoke won't bother us so much."

The housekeeper too could hardly wait to see the books go up in flames, but the priest insisted on reading every title aloud.

The first one the barber handed him was *Amadis of Gaul.* "Very interesting," remarked the priest. "This was the first book of chivalry ever to appear in Spain. Since it inspired all the rest, I say we should condemn it to be burned forthwith."

"But sir," the barber interrupted, "it's said to be one of the best books of its kind. Surely such a work, being unique, deserves a pardon."

"Very well," replied the priest. "We'll spare it for the nonce.

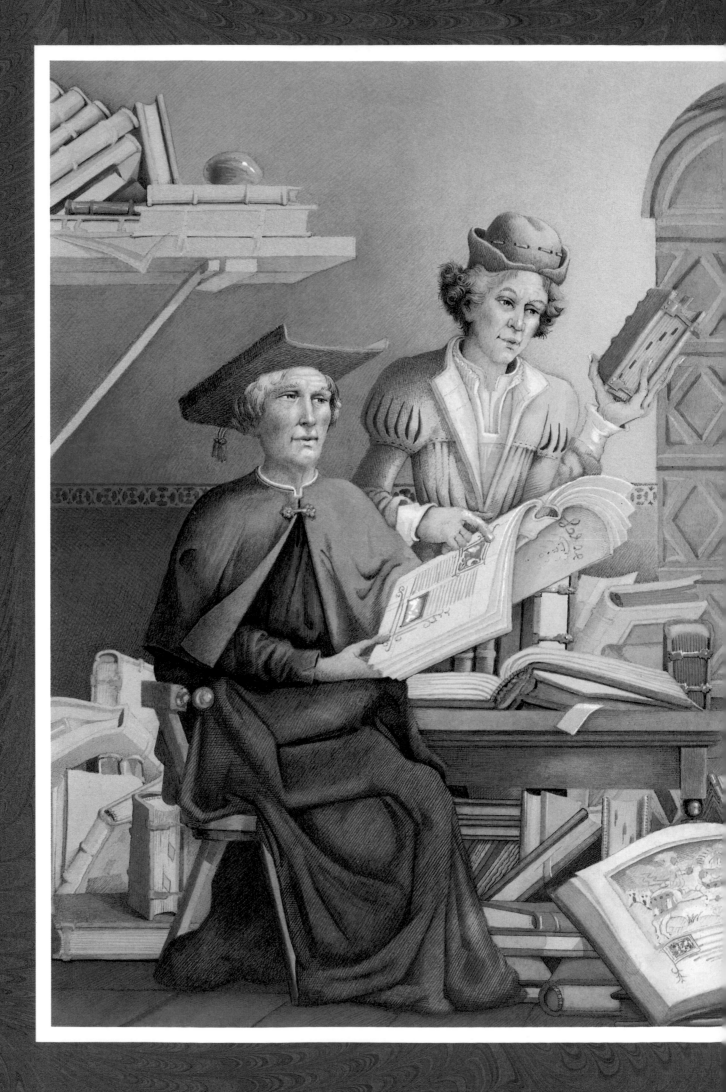

But let me see that other one you're holding."

"This," said the barber, "is *The Adventures of Esplandion.* It's the story of Amadis's son."

"Away with it, Mistress Housekeeper! Straight onto the pyre! The father's fame won't save the son."

This task the housekeeper performed with zeal, and poor Esplandion went sailing out the window.

"Next," said the priest.

"The next one," said the barber, "is *Amadis of Greece.* This stack seems to hold one Amadis tale after another."

"Away with all of them," the priest decreed.

"I agree," said the barber.

"Me too," said the niece.

"Then hand them over," said the housekeeper, and she flung them from the window.

"And this," said the barber, holding up another book, "is *The Mirror of Chivalry.*"

"I know it well," the priest replied.

"I have it in Italian," said the barber, "but I don't understand a word."

"You wouldn't understand it anyway," replied the priest, whose patience was running thin. He asked the housekeeper to take the remaining books and toss them out into the courtyard. His request did not fall on deaf ears, for she was happier to feed the flames than devote herself to her daily weaving. Seizing eight books in her arms, she hurled them from the window, but in her haste she dropped one at the barber's feet. He read its name aloud: *The Story of the Famous Knight Tirant lo Blanc.*

"Good God!" the priest exclaimed. "Tirant lo Blanc! Give it here, my friend, for by my faith it is a veritable gold mine of delight. No finer book was ever made: here knights eat at tables, lie down to sleep, and even die in their own beds with their last wills and testaments, all described in remarkable style. If you don't believe me, take it home and read it for yourself."

"I will," the barber said, "but what about these other little books?"

"These," replied the priest, picking up the first one in the stack, "are books of poetry, not chivalry. There's no need to burn them, for they're completely harmless. Their only purpose is to feed the soul."

"Really, Sir Priest!" the niece exclaimed. "I'm surprised at you! Suppose my dear uncle recovers from his bout of chivalry only to fall prey to poetry, which is not only incurable but highly catching?"

"The girl is right," replied the priest. "There's nothing for it but to hand them all over to the housekeeper's strong arm. And don't ask why or we'll never see the light of day."

"Now this one," said the barber, holding up a meaty book, "is *A Treasury of Verse.*"

"Ah," said the priest. "Hold on to it. The author is a friend of mine and has written even finer books than that."

"And this is *The Poems of Lopez Maldonado.*"

"He too is a friend of mine," the priest replied. "You should hear him read his poems aloud. What music! True, some of them run on a bit too long, but since when do quality and quantity go hand in hand? Keep him with the others. And this?"

"*The Galatea,* by Miguel de Cervantes."

"Well, well, well. A good friend of mine, Cervantes is, though better schooled in troubles than in verse. His book shows great originality, but he doesn't develop his ideas. We'll have to see how he fares with the second half he's promised to write. Maybe then he'll get the recognition he deserves. Meanwhile, keep it locked up in your room."

"With pleasure," said the barber.

Just then Don Quixote began to shout, and they cut short their examination of the remaining books, which were consigned to the flames with no further ado.

When they reached Don Quixote's room, he had gotten

out of bed and was careening about, ranting and raving and jabbing at the air, as wide awake as if he had never been asleep. They wrapped their arms around him and steered him back to his bed.

"My dear Sir Turpin," he said to the priest when he had calmed down, "It is a shame that we of the Twelve Peers should let these commoners carry off the prize when we ourselves have been victorious."

"Hush, my friend," the priest replied. "Today's loss is tomorrow's gain, and you must first tend to your health. You must be dreadfully tired, if not grievously wounded."

"Wounded I am not," said Don Quixote, "but bruised and battered beyond a shadow of a doubt. That Roldan came at me with half an oak tree. But as sure as I'm Reinaldo, he'll get what he deserves as soon as I can leave this bed. In the meantime, bring me something to eat, which will shore up my strength, and leave all acts of vengeance up to me."

They did as he bade and brought him some food. In no time at all he was as sound asleep as he had been before, and they stood watching him with open mouths, amazed as ever by his madness.

That night the housekeeper burned all the books she had thrown into the yard. Some of them deserved to be preserved forever, but bad luck and the priest's laziness dispatched them to a crueler fate. Once again, as the old proverb says, the innocent paid for the guilty.

While Don Quixote slept, the priest and the barber walled up the entrance to his library. Out of sight, out of mind, they hoped; without his books, perhaps he would forget his love of chivalry.

Just as they expected, the first thing he did when he woke up was jump to his feet and run to find his books. He looked all over the house, and finally the housekeeper explained that his entire collection had been spirited away by a magician. Don

Quixote was not convinced. In any event, he spent the next two weeks at home, entertaining the priest and the barber with all sorts of stories, arguing that what the world needed was a new supply of knights, and claiming that he would single-handedly revive the age of chivalry. Sometimes the priest argued against him and sometimes he gave in, hoping sooner or later to bring him to his senses.

Meanwhile, however, Don Quixote was talking to one of his neighbors (a good man though a little thick between the ears) in hopes of persuading him to be his squire. He promised and prodded, and prodded and promised, and even offered to make him governor of any isles he might win in knightly combat, until at long last Sancho Panza (for that was the man's name) agreed to leave his wife and children and enlist as Don Quixote's squire.

Sancho saddled his donkey and filled his saddlebags with food. Don Quixote fixed his shield and helmet and packed a few clean shirts. Then, without saying goodbye to Sancho's wife and children or to Don Quixote's housekeeper and niece, they slipped away one evening under cover of darkness. They rode all night, and by daybreak they had gone so far they knew no one would

ever find them. Sancho Panza talked of nothing else but the time when he would be a governor and his children princesses and princes.

A few hours later, they rode onto a plain with thirty or forty windmills etched against the sky.

"Our luck is even better than I expected!" Don Quixote exclaimed, turning to his squire. "I'm going to attack those mighty giants and slay them in their tracks."

"What giants?" said Sancho Panza.

"The ones up there with the long arms!"

"Those aren't giants, sir," Sancho replied. "They're windmills, and what you call their arms are blades. When there's a breeze they catch it and make the millstone turn."

"The problem with you, Sancho, is that you don't know a giant when you see one. If you're too scared to watch, stand over there and say your prayers while I finish them off."

Digging his spurs into Rocinante's side and ignoring Sancho's cries, he charged straight toward the windmills. "Flee not, base cowards," he shouted from his saddle, "for but one knight assails you!"

At that moment a slight wind rose up and the great blades began to turn. "I don't care how many arms you have!" Don Quixote roared. Commending his soul to his lady Dulcinea, he raised his shield and lunged head-on, striking his lance against the lowest blade of the first windmill. But the blade, gathering speed as it rose, dashed his lance to pieces, lifting both horse and rider high in the air, then hurling them down onto the plain.

Sancho Panza rushed to help them. "Good God!" he cried when he saw that neither Don Quixote nor his horse could move. "I told you they were windmills."

"Hush, Sancho!" said Don Quixote, looking back across the plain. And he explained that the same magician who had robbed him of his books and library had turned the giants into windmills to deprive him of his victory. "But in the end," he added, "my sword will prevail over his black heart."

Sancho helped him back onto poor Rocinante, whose shoulders had been thrown out of joint, and they rode on. By this point it was time to eat. Don Quixote had lost his appetite, so Sancho ate alone, digging into his saddlebags and raising a bottle of wine to his lips from time to time until he had recovered his high spirits.

That night they bedded down under some trees. Sancho slept like a log, his stomach full of food and drink. But Don Quixote lay awake the way a good knight should, thinking of his Dulcinea.

The next morning they started out again toward a place called Lapice, where, said Don Quixote, they would find themselves up to their elbows in adventures.

Not long after they set out, two black-robed monks rode into view on mules as big as camels. They held parasols above their heads and wore special riding masks to protect them from the dust. Behind them came a horse-drawn coach inside which, as they later learned, sat a lady on her way to Seville to meet her husband, who had been named to an important post in the New World. Two muleteers on foot brought up the rear.

"I may be wrong," said Don Quixote, "but something tells me this is going to be the greatest adventure ever seen. I wager there's a kidnapped princess in that coach."

"This is going to be even worse than the windmills," Sancho groaned. "Those men are Benedictine monks, sir, and the people in the coach are probably just ordinary travelers. Don't let the Devil blind you to what's right before your nose."

"The trouble with you, Sancho," Don Quixote replied, "is that you don't know a real adventure when you see one."

So saying, he rode forward and stopped in the middle of the road.

"Bedeviled louts!" he shouted. "Release the princesses inside your coach or prepare to meet your death at once!"

The monks dropped their reins and stared at the strange

man before them. "We are neither bedeviled nor louts, sir, but Benedictine monks going peacefully about our business."

"Liars!" shouted Don Quixote, spurring Rocinante on and lunging at the first of the two monks, who was knocked to the ground. The second one, seeing what had happened to the first, dug his heels into his towering mount and disappeared across a field.

Sancho Panza leapt from his ass and began to strip the first monk of his habit. When the two muleteers asked what he was doing, he explained that he was taking his portion of the spoils due his master, Don Quixote, who had just bested their own in knightly combat. The pair had no idea what spoils were, but seeing Don Quixote engaged in conversation with the occupants of the coach, they fell on Sancho Panza and beat him to a pulp. Then they helped the frightened monk back onto his mule and watched as he and his brother, who was waiting for him at a safe remove, vanished over the horizon, crossing themselves as profusely as if the Devil himself were at their backs.

Meanwhile, Don Quixote was speaking with the lady in the coach.

"Now may thy ladyship dispose as she sees fit, for thy abductor's pride lies toppled in the dust. Know this: he that set thee free is Don Quixote de la Mancha, knight errant and captive of the peerless beauty Dulcinea del Toboso, who in return for his good deed asks only that you travel to El Toboso to tell his lady how he saved thee in the hour of thy distress."

But no sooner had he finished speaking than one of the coachmen stepped forward and told him to get moving. "If you were a knight..." Don Quixote began.

"Am I not?" the coachman countered.

"Slave!"

"Liar!"

"I'll show you what I am!" cried Don Quixote, drawing his sword. And before anyone could stop him, he had rushed at his opponent, determined to stop him in his tracks. But the coachman followed suit and the two stood poised to strike, their swords over their heads. For a moment heaven and earth came to a standstill, but suddenly the coachman lunged, bringing his sword down on Don Quixote's shoulder and slicing off half of his helmet along with a piece of his left ear.

Who can describe the rage that rose in Don Quixote's heart when he realized what had happened? Or how he managed to straighten himself in his stirrups, grab his sword in both his hands, and strike the coachman in the head, until the poor man was spewing blood from ears and nose and mouth, as if a whole mountain had caved in on him?

Meanwhile, the ladies in the coach, who had been looking on in wordless horror, came running up to Don Quixote and begged him to spare their coachman's life.

"But of course, my dears," Don Quixote replied in the haughtiest voice he could produce. "On one condition. Your friend must travel to the town of El Toboso, where he will present himself before my lady Dulcinea, who will do with him as she sees fit."

The terrified ladies agreed to this request without wondering who Dulcinea was or what Don Quixote really meant.

"Now I ask you," Don Quixote said, turning to his squire, who had managed to peel himself up from the ground, "have you ever read of a knight with more spirit in his heart, more strength in his arm, more breath in his lungs, or more skill in toppling his opponents?"

"To tell you the truth," Sancho replied, "I've never read anything at all, because I don't know how to read or write. What I do know is that I've never served a braver master in my life. Now let me treat your wounds, for blood is rushing from your ear."

Don Quixote almost swooned when he saw his bloody helmet. "I swear anew," he announced, "to lead the life of a knight errant until I have won another helmet as fine as this. Believe me, these aren't idle words: I speak, of course, of the helmet of Mambrino."

"I wish you wouldn't swear so much," said Sancho Panza. "It's not good for your health. Besides, there are hardly any armed men on the road these days, let alone one who wears a helmet. All we ever see are mule drivers."

"You're wrong, my friend," said Don Quixote. "Two hours from now we will have come across more men in arms than most people see in a whole lifetime."

"I hope you're right, sir, and that it won't be long before you win that isle or island you keep telling me about."

Don Quixote explained that battles fought on country roads did not generally yield isles, but assured his squire that in due time Sancho would not only be a governor, but something greater still. "If worse comes to worst, there's always Denmark," he added. "It might be just the place for you, and besides, it's inland. But let's leave that to time. By the way, do we have anything to eat?"

"There's an onion and some cheese and a few chunks of bread. Hardly fare for a knight as valiant as yourself," said Sancho Panza.

"If you'd read as many tales as I have, Sancho," said Don Quixote, "you'd know knights errant had to be content with what they found. After all, they spent most of their time out in the woods, just like you and I, and their food was simple country fare like ours. So don't worry about what I ought to eat, or try to reinvent the world from scratch."

"Forgive me," Sancho replied, "From now on I'll be sure to bring along dried fruit. Of course, I'll pack something more substantial for myself—like chicken."

"I didn't mean they ate *only* what they found," said Don Quixote.

With that, Sancho reached into his saddlebags. After they had eaten their small meal they rode off in search of a place to spend the night, but the sun and their hopes faded faster than they had expected. Sancho was disappointed not to reach a village, but Don Quixote was happy to sleep beneath the open sky. It made him feel more like a knight.

The next morning, after riding for hours in a thick forest, they came upon a gentle meadow that seemed to call out to them to stop at once and spend the hottest hours of the day on the cool, enchanting grass.

Sancho and Don Quixote left Rocinante and the ass to graze untethered while they turned to the provisions in their saddlebags. But as luck and the Devil would have it, just as master and servant were sitting down to enjoy their midday meal, Rocinante noticed a herd of Galician mares in the very clearing where he had been set loose and flew off in their direction like a light. The lady horses, however, were more interested in nibbling their grass, and received him with a mix of hooves and teeth so powerful that before Rocinante realized what had hit him, he was standing almost naked in the middle of the field, his saddle gone and his girth torn. As if that wasn't enough, the men in charge of the herd came running toward him with long wooden staves and beat him almost senseless.

By this point Don Quixote and Sancho Panza arrived, huffing and puffing after witnessing the assault on Rocinante from afar.

"As anyone can see," said Don Quixote, "these are vile, lowborn men, which means that you can help avenge the outrage they have just inflicted on Rocinante."

"Surely you jest," Sancho replied. "There are more than twenty of them and only two of us—or should I say one and a half?"

"I'm as good as a hundred," proclaimed Don Quixote, drawing his sword and immediately dealing one of the herdsmen a deep gash in the neck. Inspired by his example, Sancho quickly followed suit.

But when the herdsmen saw themselves so brutally treated by a mere two men, they grabbed their wooden staves and lit into Sancho and Don Quixote, who went reeling to the ground, landing, of all places, right at Rocinante's feet. Realizing that they had gotten a bit carried away, the herdsmen rounded up their horses and beat a fast retreat, leaving the two adventurers in sorry shape and an even sorrier state of mind.

The first one to recover his senses was Sancho Panza. "Don Quixote!" he cried in a pitiful and wounded voice. "My Don Quixote!"

"What is it, my brother Sancho?" Don Quixote replied in the same feeble tone.

"How long do you think it will be before we can stand up?"

"For myself," said Don Quixote, who was as bruised as a tomato, "I know there is no end in sight. I should never have raised my sword against men who weren't knights. That's why the lord of battles saw fit to punish me—for breaking the laws of chivalry. Make no mistake, Sancho. Next time, you'll strike the first blow. Of course, if it's knights we're up against, I'll do the honors. I don't have to tell you what this strong right arm of mine can do."

Sancho Panza was not impressed. "Sir," he said, "I am a meek and gentle man, a man of peace. I have a wife and children to look after. Let me warn you (since I can't give you orders): I will never draw my sword again against either knight or knave.

Furthermore, with God as my witness, I hereby forgive all and any offenses that have been or might yet be committed against me by any man, whether rich or poor, highborn or low, nobleman or commoner, with no exception."

"Ah, Panza," said Don Quixote, clutching his bruised ribs, "had I but breath enough to show you the error of your ways. Come here, you fool, and listen closely! Suppose the winds of fortune suddenly shifted in our favor and we finally sailed into possession of one of those isles I've been promising you. And let's say I made you governor. Why, you'd make a mess of everything! You know, Sancho, in kingdoms and territories that have just been conquered, the natives are never terribly enchanted with the new authorities, much less with their new ruler. So they try to turn things upside down and return things to their former state. That means that you must rule with intelligence and have the courage to defend yourself in an emergency."

"I wish I had the intelligence and courage of which you speak," said Sancho, "but to be perfectly honest, right now I'm more in need of bandages than sermons."

"Fortune always leaves a trapdoor open in disasters," Don Quixote replied. "For example, now we'll use your little mount instead of Rocinante to take me to some castle where they'll treat my wound. Which reminds me of old Silenus, tutor to the god of laughter, who rode an ass just like your own when he entered the city of the hundred gates."

"I'm sure he did," Sancho replied, "But there's a big difference between riding and being thrown across the ass's back like a bag of dung."

"Wounds received in battle," answered Don Quixote, "bestow honor rather than deny it. So, my dear friend Panza, enough of all your talk. Get up as best you can and pitch me up onto your ass however you will. Let's be off before night overtakes us in this wilderness."

Sancho, emitting thirty wails, sixty sighs, and one hundred and twenty aye, aye, aye's at the man who had brought him to this pass, started to raise himself from the ground. He was bent like a bow, and got stuck part of the way up. Even so, he managed to harness his ass and lay Don Quixote across its back. Then, helping Rocinante to his feet, he tied him to the ass's tail and set off toward where he thought the highway lay.

They had gone only two miles when luck, who was leading them from good to better, brought them within sight of an inviting inn. Sancho was delighted, but Don Quixote insisted that it was a castle, and they argued back and forth about it right through the gates and up to the front door, where they were warmly welcomed by the innkeeper and his wife.

When the innkeeper asked why Don Quixote was sprawled face down across the ass, Sancho made light of what had happened, explaining that his master had fallen from a rock and bruised his ribs. The innkeeper's wife, a woman of unusual compassion and considerable insight, immediately assigned her daughter, a comely girl, to take special care of their new guest.

The daughter was assisted by a flat-faced servant girl named Maritornes, who although she was only three feet tall and as blind in one eye as she was bleary in the other, made up in charm what she lacked in appearance.

After helping her young mistress settle Don Quixote into a wretched bed in an attic that had once been a hayloft, Maritornes held a lantern while the innkeeper's wife poulticed Don Quixote from head to toe.

"By the way," Sancho said when they were done, "save a little of that gauze. You never know when you might need it. Actually, my back is bothering me a little too."

"Then you must have fallen too," replied the hostess.

"I did not," said Sancho Panza. "But I ache so much from the shock of seeing my master fall that I feel as if I'd received a thousand thrashings."

"That's happened to me too," said the young girl. "I often dream that I'm falling from a tower, and when I awake I'm as

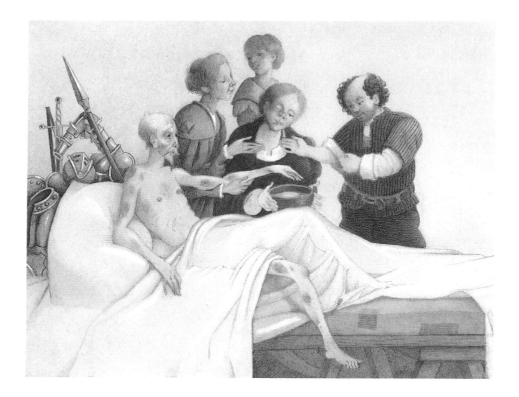

bruised and battered as if I had really fallen."

"But I wasn't dreaming," Sancho said. "I was wider awake than I am now, and I still have nearly as many bruises as my master Don Quixote."

"What did you say his name was?" asked Maritornes.

"Don Quixote de la Mancha," Sancho Panza replied. "He's a knight errant, one of the best and bravest the world has seen in many a long year."

"What's a knight errant?" asked Maritornes.

"What—were you born yesterday?" Sancho exclaimed. "Well, if you don't know, I'll tell you. To make a long story short, a knight errant is battered one day and an emperor the next. Today he's the neediest, most wretched creature in the world and tomorrow he has kingdoms galore to bestow upon his faithful squire."

Don Quixote suddenly sat up in bed. "Beauteous lady," he said, taking the hostess's hand, "thou mayest consider thyself fortunate for having sheltered my person in thy castle. I shall carry forever inscribed in my memory the service thou hast rendered me tonight. Would that love held me not so in thrall to my lady Dulcinea but that this lovely damsel might be the mistress of my will."

The hostess was bewildered by the knight errant's speech, which might have been in Greek for all she knew. Still, she understood enough to tell that he was complimenting her. She thanked him with her ordinary innkeeper's words and she and her daughter said good night, leaving Maritornes behind to tend to Sancho.

By the next morning, Sancho was still a bundle of aches and pains, but Don Quixote was in fine fettle and eager to pursue his next adventure. While more than twenty other guests stood watching, he saddled Rocinante and helped Sancho up onto his ass. Then he climbed onto his horse and addressed the innkeeper, who was standing in the doorway. "Many and great are the favors you have extended to me in this great castle, my lord. If I can repay you by taking vengeance on any man who may have wronged you, know that my calling is none other than to help those who cannot help themselves. Search your memory. If there be anything along these lines, you have only to say the word and I promise by my oath of knighthood to faithfully execute your wishes."

The innkeeper replied in the same quiet vein. "Sir Knight, I do not need Your Worship to avenge me of anything. I am perfectly capable of doing so myself. All I ask is that you pay your bill, which includes dinner and bed for you and your squire as well as straw and fodder for your mounts."

"Then this is an inn?" asked Don Quixote.

"And a very respectable one," the innkeeper replied.

"You don't say," said Don Quixote. "I was convinced it was a castle. But if it's an inn, you should at least forgive my bill. Surely you don't expect me to go against the order of knights errant, who never pay for their lodgings or any other service in places where they stay the night and who rightly and richly deserve the welcome they receive. Just think what wear and tear they suffer as they go about the world, assailed by the sky's ingratitude and every inconvenience of the earth."

"That," replied the innkeeper, "is no business of mine. Pay me what you owe and keep your accounts of knighthood to yourself. The only thing that counts with me is what goes into my pocket."

"You're a blockhead and a lousy hosteler to boot," said Don Quixote. And spurring Rocinante on, he sped from the inn so fast that nobody could stop him and rode as far as he could without looking behind him.

After the hasty departure of his guest, the innkeeper turned to Sancho Panza, but Sancho declared that as squire to a knight errant, the same rule and reason held for him as for his master. This sent the innkeeper into a fury. If Sancho wouldn't pay of his own will, he said, he'd pay in some other, more unpleasant, way. But Sancho was unmoved. Not on his account would the great and ancient custom of knight errantry be lost, nor would future generations of squires have him to blame if such a righteous rule were broken.

Alas, as fate would have it, among the other guests at the inn were four wool-carders from Segovia, three needle-makers from Cordoba, and two traders from the market of Seville—as lively, as well-meaning, as mischievous, and as playful a crowd as ever walked the earth. All nine of them rushed up to Sancho, pulled him from his ass, threw him on a blanket, and began to toss him up and down.

The cries of the poor wretch were loud enough to reach the ears of Don Quixote, who stopped in his tracks, thinking some new adventure was upon him. When he recognized his squire's voice, he immediately turned Rocinante back toward the inn, where he saw Sancho rising and falling through the air with such consummate grace that if he hadn't been so angry he would certainly have burst out laughing.

Unfortunately, Don Quixote was unable to dismount his horse because of all his bruises. He began to curse Sancho's tossers with words too vile to be recorded, but they ignored him, continuing to laugh and toss, toss and laugh, just as hapless Sancho continued to rise and fall, fall and rise, his cries mixed now with threats and now with pitiful entreaties, all of which fell on deaf ears, for his tormentors relented only when they were too tired to go on.

Finally, they brought him his ass, threw him upon it, and wrapped him in his coat. The good-hearted Maritornes brought him a jug of ice-cold water she had just drawn from the well, but when Sancho tasted it, he refused to drink another sip, begging her to bring him a carafe of wine. This she produced forthwith, paying for it out of her own pocket.

After he had drunk his fill, Sancho dug his heels into his ass's sides and rode out through the front gate, pleased that he had had his way without paying a cent, although his shoulders had borne some of the cost.

The innkeeper wanted to bolt the door behind him, but the blanket tossers refused. When it came right down to it, it was all the same to them whether Don Quixote was or wasn't one of the Knights of the Round Table.

"In my opinion, sir," said Sancho as they rode along, "all our troubles stem from the fact that you broke your solemn oath as a knight errant. You swore not to eat bread off a tablecloth or do all sorts of other things until you had obtained Mambrino's helmet. Don't you remember?"

"To tell you the truth," Don Quixote replied, "I had quite forgotten. In fact, if you had remembered to remind me, chances are you wouldn't have been shaken up and down like a rattle on that blanket. But don't worry—the law of chivalry works in mysterious ways."

That day they rode very slowly and talked so much that darkness and hunger overtook them before they found a place to stay. As they peered into the pitch-black night, they saw a swirl of lights that looked more like stars in motion than anything else.

Sancho was terrified, and Don Quixote was scarcely a whit happier at the strange sight.

As the lights drew closer, Sancho began to shake as if he had swallowed mercury, and Don Quixote's hair stood straight up from his head. "Something tells me," he said, "that I'm going to need every ounce of courage I can muster."

"Oh me, oh my!" Sancho exclaimed. "If this has anything to do with ghosts, how will I bear up?"

"Don't you worry about ghosts," said Don Quixote. "I'll see to it they don't go near you."

"What if they put a spell on you?"

"Sancho, please. I promise not to let you down."

They soon made out a number of white shapes, at which Sancho Panza's courage completely failed him and his teeth began to chatter. His terror increased when they were able to discern some twenty horsemen in white robes, each holding a torch and each muttering under his breath. Behind them came a litter draped in black followed by six riders swathed in black down to their mules' feet, for it was clear from the animals' slow pace that they were not horses.

This strange vision at such a time of night and in such an abandoned place would have been enough to strike fear not only into Sancho's heart but his master's as well, except that Don Quixote was convinced it was a scene from one of his books. He fancied the litter a bier on which some knight lay dead or grievously wounded and thought that he alone had been assigned to avenge whatever injury the poor man might have suffered. So, with no further ado, he lowered his lance, drew himself up tall in the saddle, and with noble bearing and dispatch stationed himself in the middle of the road, directly in the path of the oncoming troupe.

"Halt," he called out as they approached, "and say who you are, whence you come, whither you go, and what you are transporting on that bier. For by all appearances you have either done or been done some terrible harm, the nature of which I must know at once so I can either punish you or right the wrong that you have suffered."

"We're in a hurry," one of the figures in white robes replied, spurring his mule. "The inn is still a long way off. We don't have time to answer all your questions."

But Don Quixote grabbed his bridle and held him fast. "You will if you know what's good for you. And watch your manners. Either answer my questions, or we are at war."

The mule was so frightened at having her bridle seized that she reared up on her hind legs and threw her rider to the ground. One of the men on foot began to curse Don Quixote, who immediately charged, gravely wounding one of the pallbearers. From there it was a wonder to behold how swiftly he wheeled about, attacking now one, then another of the white-clad host. Rocinante too flew from side to side as if he had sprouted wings. In minutes most of the men had fled to a nearby field, brandishing their blazing torches like a band of revelers rushing from some masquerade. The pallbearers, however, weighed down by their robes, were unable to move, and as they flailed about trying to escape, Don Quixote gave them a dreadful drubbing. They were sure he was a devil sent from hell itself to steal the corpse they were accompanying to its final resting place.

Sancho, meanwhile, watched from the sidelines, wide-eyed with admiration. "Clearly," he said to himself, "my master Don Quixote is as bold and courageous as he claims."

In the flickering light of a single torch still burning on the ground, Don Quixote made out the figure of the man who had first been toppled from his mount. Pointing the tip of his lance at the man's face, he ordered him to surrender on pain of death. "I have already surrendered," the wounded man replied, explaining that his leg was broken and begging Don Quixote to spare his life. He was a student priest, he said, and had already taken his first orders.

"What the Devil brings you to a place like this," thundered Don Quixote, "if you are a churchman?"

"Bad luck, sir," said the student.

"Well, let me warn you: even worse luck awaits you unless you are prepared to answer all my questions."

"Don't worry," replied the student, introducing himself as Alonso Lopez and promptly meeting Don Quixote's request. "I was on my way to Segovia with eleven other priests—the men with the torches who have run away—to bury the gentleman whose body is lying on that litter."

"Who killed him?"

"The Lord Himself, sir, through a terrible pox that struck him dead."

"In that case," Don Quixote mused, "I'm no longer under any obligation to avenge his death. There's nothing for it but to shrug my shoulders, just as I would do if He killed me. Still, I would have you know that I am Don Quixote de la Mancha, and that my calling and profession is to roam the world avenging wrongs and righting injuries."

"I can't imagine what you mean," remarked the student, "for I was straight and now I'm crooked, with a leg that will never be put right again."

"That, Sir Alonso Lopez," Don Quixote replied, "is because you took it upon yourselves to ride out in the dark in those awful robes, muttering prayers and waving torches that made you look like ghosts. I had no choice but to fulfill my knightly duty by attacking you."

"Be that as it may," the student said, "I entreat your worship, Sir Knight Errant, to help me up from underneath this mule. My leg is stuck between the stirrup and the saddle."

"Why didn't you tell me that before?" asked Don Quixote, calling for Sancho Panza to give him a hand. But Sancho was busy rifling a saddlebag he had removed from one of the priests' mules, which was packed with every sort of delectable provision. Making a bag of his overcoat, Sancho crammed it full of victuals and hoisted it up onto his ass. Only then was he prepared to heed his master's call.

After the young priest was free, Don Quixote handed him his torch and sent him after his companions, begging him to apologize for the harm he had had no choice but to inflict upon them.

"And if they ask who did them the honor," Sancho chimed in, "tell them it was the famous Don Quixote of La Mancha, also known as the Knight of the Sad Countenance."

With that the young priest rode off, and Don Quixote asked Sancho what had led him to call him the Knight of the Sad Countenance, especially just then.

"Because," said Sancho Panza, "seeing you in the glow of that torch, I noticed what a worn-out face you've had of late. I don't know whether it's because you're so tired or because all your teeth have been knocked out."

"More likely," said Don Quixote, "the sage who is writing the story of my life thought I ought to have a title, like all knights of yore. There was the Knight of the Burning Sword, the Knight of the Unicorn, the Knight of the Damsels, the Knight of the Phoenix, of the Griffin—even a Knight of Death. Those names were known around the world. I'm sure that's why the writer of this book put the name Knight of the Sad Countenance into your mouth. That is how I shall be called from this day on, and to insure a perfect fit, I intend to have an extremely woeful face painted on my shield as soon as possible."

"There's no point wasting time and money on a painting, sir," said Sancho Panza. "Believe me, your face speaks for itself. All you have to do is lift your visor, and anyone who sees it will immediately call you the Knight of the Sad Countenance."

Don Quixote laughed, but even so, he resolved to go by his new name and have his shield painted accordingly.

Despite the late hour, he wanted to peek at the corpse to see if it was a skeleton, but Sancho insisted it was time to go. "The dead to their graves and the living to their dinner," he proclaimed, spurring on his mount, and Don Quixote followed him into the jet-black night without a word.

They rode out between two hills and soon found themselves in a wide, secluded valley. Sancho jumped down from his ass, opened one of the hampers they had taken from the dead man's party, and spread its contents on the ground, where they sat down to eat their breakfast, lunch, and dinner all rolled into one. The only thing missing was something to drink, for there was neither wine nor water and their throats were parched with thirst. But the grass they were sitting on was so green and thick that Sancho said there had to be a spring or river close at hand.

Don Quixote thought that was a reasonable idea, so they began to grope their way across the meadow, leading Rocinante by the reins and the donkey by the halter. Before they had gone two hundred steps they heard the roar of rushing water, which they imagined must be falling from some huge, imposing rocks. This greatly cheered them, but when they stopped to listen, they heard another sound that quickly doused their spirits, especially Sancho's, since he was a fearful, fainthearted soul to begin with. This second noise, a series of deafening blows accompanied by a loud clanking of iron and chains, would have struck terror into any other heart but Don Quixote's.

The night, as already mentioned, was dark, and they happened to have stopped beneath a stand of trees whose leaves rustled in the gentle breeze. The combination of the solitude, the setting, the darkness, the thundering water, and the rustling leaves filled them with dread and horror, especially when the blows did not let up, the wind die down, or the sun rise. Besides, they didn't have the foggiest idea of where they were. But Don Quixote, summoning his ever-present courage, leapt onto Rocinante's back, grabbed his shield, and waved his lance high in the air.

"Sancho, my friend," he cried, "all that we see and hear before us only quickens my soul and rouses my heart to embark the more quickly on this next adventure, difficult and harrowing as it may be. For I am he who has been called to revive the age of chivalry. Make fast Rocinante's girths and God be with you! You shall wait for me three days, no more. If I do not appear, you may return to our village and travel thence to El Toboso, where you will tell my lady Dulcinea that her faithful knight died attempting deeds that would make him worthy of her name."

At this, Sancho began to weep the most pitiful tears in the whole world. "I left my village and my wife and children in order to serve you, fully expecting to improve my lot. And now, just when I thought my promised isle was in view, you intend to leave me all alone in this godforsaken place. It's dark now, and there's not a soul in sight. Why tempt fate? We can easily slip away and escape this danger without anyone accusing us of being cowards. Please, sir, even if you are determined to press on, at least wait till morning. For by the science I learned when I was a shepherd, dawn is less than three hours away: the Bear's muzzle is already above his head."

"How can you see head or bear or muzzle, Sancho, when it's so dark out that there's not a single star?"

"Fear has many eyes, sir. Besides, it's logical to think that daybreak can't be far away."

"Near or far," said Don Quixote, "let it not be said that tears and whimpers kept me from my knightly task. I beg you, Sancho, be still. Let God watch over me and calm your fears. I'll be back soon, alive or dead."

When Sancho saw that Don Quixote would not be swayed by words or tears, he decided to use his ingenuity instead. While he was tightening Rocinante's girths, he tied the horse's forelegs together with the halter of his ass, which he managed to do so unobtrusively and perfectly that when Don Quixote tried to leave, Rocinante was unable to move forward except by awkward jumps.

"You see, Your Worship, Heaven has heard my tears and prayers and ordered Rocinante to stay put."

The more Don Quixote spurred his horse, the less he could make him move. He decided it was best to relax and wait until the sun came up or Rocinante recovered his ability to walk, whichever came first.

Sancho offered to entertain him with some stories while he waited, unless Don Quixote wished to take a little nap till daybreak. That way he would be less tired when the time came to set out on his next unparalleled adventure.

"What are you talking about?" asked Don Quixote. "Do I strike you as the sort of knight to be caught napping in the midst of danger? Sleep yourself, since you were born to, and let me do as I see fit."

"Don't be angry, Your Worship," Sancho said, putting his right hand on the pommel of Don Quixote's saddle and clasping his master's thigh without daring to move an inch, so frightened was he of the blows that continued to fall in the distance. Don Quixote asked him to tell a story, and Sancho said he would if he could manage to control his fear.

"Once upon a time," he began, "in a village of Extremadura, there was a shepherd—actually a goatherd, because it was goats he shepherded, not sheep—and this shepherd, or goatherd as the case may be, was called Lope Ruiz. And this Lope Ruiz fell in love with a shepherdess whose name was Torralba, and this shepherdess Torralba was the daughter of a rich herdsman called—"

"If you go on like this," said Don Quixote, "repeating everything you say two times, you'll still be telling it the day after tomorrow."

"The way I tell it," replied Sancho Panza, "is the way everyone tells stories where I'm from. It's the only way I know."

"Very well," said Don Quixote. "Since I'm condemned to listen, tell it as you will."

"As I was saying, then," Sancho continued, "this shepherd was madly in love with the shepherdess Torralba, a plump, headstrong girl with a slightly mannish look due to the hint of a mustache. I can see her now—"

"You knew her personally?" asked Don Quixote.

"I never met her," Sancho replied, "but the friend who told me this story assured me everything about it was so true to life that I could swear I had seen it all with my own eyes. In any case, as day follows night, the love the shepherd bore the shepherdess soon turned to spite, and he decided to leave for Portugal, where he would never set eyes on her again. He crossed the plains of Extremadura and arrived with all his goats at the banks of the Guadiana River, which was almost overflowing. But as he stood there wondering what to do with his three hundred goats, he saw Torralba coming after him in hot pursuit. Fortunately, at that very moment a fisherman rowed up in a small skiff. His boat would hold only one goat at a time; still, it was the only way the shepherd and his goats could reach the other side, so the shepherd quickly struck a deal. Now listen carefully, Your Worship, and keep track of the goats as they cross over. If you lose count I'll have to stop my tale. The fisherman began to ferry them across one goat at a time. He continued back and forth, back

and forth across the river, taking first one goat, then another, then another, then another—"

"Let's just say they're all across," said Don Quixote.

"How many have already reached the other side?" asked Sancho Panza.

"How the hell should I know?" exclaimed Don Quixote.

"You see? I told you to keep track. Now I can't go on."

"Is the exact number really so important that your story falls apart without it?"

"No, Your Worship. But when I asked how many goats had crossed so far and you said you didn't know, the rest of the tale flew clear out of my head."

"My word," said Don Quixote. "You've told me one of the most original tales I've ever heard. This awful din must have stirred up your imagination."

By this point dawn was fast approaching, and Sancho carefully unfettered Rocinante. The horse immediately began to paw the ground, which Don Quixote took as a good omen for his upcoming adventure.

As the sun began to rise and things became visible in the dim light, Don Quixote once again took leave of Sancho Panza, instructing him to wait three days, at the end of which, if he had not returned, he should assume the worst. He reminded Sancho of the message he was to take his lady Dulcinea and assured him that, whatever happened, he would be paid in full. If, however, God should bring him through the coming danger safe and sound, the promised isle was a certainty. All this made Sancho weep afresh, and he decided not to leave his master until he had seen the entire business through to its proper ending and conclusion.

Don Quixote was moved by his squire's tears, but his determination was unshaken; and so, doing his utmost to hide his fear, he set off in the direction of the thundering water and deafening blows.

Sancho followed him on foot, leading his donkey by the halter. They had gone only a few paces when they entered a small clearing that brought them face to face with a sheer cliff down which an avalanche of water was cascading. At the foot of the cliff was a cluster of ramshackle houses that looked more like ruins than dwellings, from whose midst, they quickly realized, the dreadful din was rising.

Rocinante started at the noise, but Don Quixote calmed him down and they continued toward the houses. The knight commended himself to his lady, imploring her to look kindly on his formidable task; then, just to be on the safe side, he also commended himself to God. Sancho, meanwhile, stayed close upon his master's heels, bending down from time to time to peer ahead between Rocinante's legs.

They must have gone another hundred paces when, rounding the corner of a rock, they came upon the unmistakable cause of the ghastly and, to their ears, horrifying sounds that had kept them in such mortal terror through the night. Which turned out to be nothing more than six ordinary textile presses whose hammers and pistons were making all that noise.

Sancho looked at Don Quixote and Don Quixote looked at Sancho, whose apple cheeks were about to burst with laughter. At this Don Quixote himself began to laugh, whereupon Sancho could no longer contain himself and let go with such a gale of merriment that he had to hold his sides. Four times he calmed himself down, and four times he began to laugh anew, just as violently as before.

"'Sancho, my friend,'" he said in mockery, "'all that we see and hear before us only quickens my soul and rouses my heart to embark the more quickly on this next adventure, difficult and harrowing as it may be. For I am he who has been called to revive the age of chivalry. Make fast Rocinante's girths and God be with you!'" And he continued, repeating most of what Don Quixote had said when they first heard the fearful blows.

When Don Quixote realized that Sancho was making fun of him, he grew so angry that he raised his lance and dealt him two blows that, had they hit him on the head instead of on the shoulder, would have released the knight forever from paying his squire's wages.

"Easy does it, Your Worship—I was just kidding," Sancho said with great humility, afraid his master might get carried away.

"You may be kidding," Don Quixote replied, "but I, you can be sure, am not."

"I admit I laughed a bit too much," said Sancho, "but tell me—now that we're safe again, isn't it amusing that we were so scared, and doesn't it make a wonderful story?"

"It may be worth laughing at," replied Don Quixote, "but as to turning it into a story, not everyone knows how to find the point of what they hear."

"You certainly found the point of your lance and knew how

to aim it. Oh well. As the saying goes, 'He who hurls the sharpest dart holds you closest to his heart.'"

"Fate may prove you right," said Don Quixote. "But see that from now on you hold your tongue and exercise restraint when you address me; for in all the countless books of chivalry I've read, I've never come across a squire who talked as much as you do. Besides, by now you must have realized that there has to be a line between master and servant and between knight and squire. There has to be much more respect between us and less humor."

"What you say is reasonable enough," said Sancho Panza, "but just in case your promises fall through, I'd like to know what kind of wages squires made back then and whether they were paid each month or by the day."

"I don't think squires ever worked for wages," replied Don Quixote, "but you can rest assured as to my favors, for I've already written you into my will. We don't know how chivalry will fare in this calamitous age of ours, and I wouldn't want my soul to suffer in the next life on account of such a trivial affair as this. I don't need to tell you that there is no lot more perilous than a knight errant's."

"Indeed," said Sancho Panza. "Especially since the noise of an ordinary textile press was enough to alarm so valiant a knight errant as yourself. However, from now on I promise not to use my lips to mock you, but only to pay you homage as my natural lord and master."

"For that," replied Don Quixote, "you shall live long and well on the face of the earth; for we are meant to honor our masters as we would our parents."

By the next morning a light rain had begun to fall. As the road turned to the right, Don Quixote caught sight of a man on horseback with something on his head that shone like gold.

"What did I tell you, Sancho?" he said. "When one door shuts another opens. If I'm not mistaken, that man riding toward us is wearing the helmet of Mambrino, which as you know I've sworn to recapture."

"I wouldn't be so sure," Sancho replied. "If I could freely speak my mind, I might convince you that Your Worship is in error."

"What? How dare you, impudent traitor! Do you not see that knight coming toward us on a dappled steed with a gold helmet on his head?"

"What I see and surmise," said Sancho Panza, "is a man on a gray donkey just like mine, with something shiny on his head."

"And that," said Don Quixote, "is Mambrino's helmet. Stand aside and let me handle this alone. You'll see how swiftly I win the helmet of my dreams."

Now the true story of the helmet, the horse, and the horseman goes something like this. In that corner of Spain there were two villages, one too small to have its own apothecary shop or barber, the other large enough for one of each. Thus, the barber of the large town was obliged to cut hair in the smaller, as well as tend the sick, which was part of a barber's job back then. To this very end, in fact, the barber from the large town was on his way to the small one, with his brass shaving basin tucked beneath his arm. But as fate would have it, it began to rain, and the barber, fearing that his new hat would be ruined, put the shaving basin on his head. His mount was a gray donkey, just as Sancho said, which explains why Don Quixote thought he saw a dappled steed, a golden helmet, and a knight.

No sooner did the hapless man draw near than Don Quixote urged Rocinante to a canter, intending to run him through. "Defend yourself," he cried, lowering his lance, "or freely give me what is mine!"

With this apparition bearing down on him, the barber saw no escape from Don Quixote's lance except to roll from his ass and tear headlong into a nearby field. Which is exactly what he did, running faster than the wind and leaving behind the cherished basin, which Don Quixote asked Sancho to retrieve.

"By God," Sancho exclaimed, turning it over in his hands, "it's a fine basin indeed, and should fetch a handsome price." And he gave it to his master.

Don Quixote put it on his head and turned it around and around searching for the visor. But he soon gave up. "The hero for whom this famous headpiece was first cast must have had an enormous head," he said. "What's worse, half of it is missing."

When Sancho heard the basin called a headpiece he could no longer keep from laughing. Still, mindful of his master's wrath, he tried to control himself.

"What are you laughing at?" asked Don Quixote.

"At the thought of that big head," Sancho replied, "crowned by such a helmet, which resembles nothing so much as an ordinary shaving basin."

"You know what I think, Sancho? I think this enchanted helmet must have fallen into the hands of people who had no idea of its true worth. In their ignorance, they melted down the other half and sold it for its weight in gold. Then they made this half in the shape of what you say resembles a barber's basin. Of course, the change is trifling to anyone who knows its origin. As soon as we come upon a blacksmith's shop I'll have it repaired so it will rival or even surpass the helmet that the god of blacksmiths crafted for the god of battle. In the meantime, I'll wear

it anyway, for something is better than nothing. Besides, it may protect me from a stoning."

"One more thing," said Sancho Panza. "What are we to do with this gray steed that looks like an ordinary gray ass? Judging by the amount of dust that poor man kicked up as he ran, he won't be coming back for it any time soon. And, by my chin, I daresay it's a handsome beast!"

"It is not my custom," Don Quixote replied, "to plunder those I vanquish, nor does the law of chivalry look favorably on the taking of one's adversary's horse, unless one's own is lost. Therefore, Sancho, leave this horse, or mule, or donkey, or whatever you think it is. As soon as its owner sees us depart, he'll return for it."

"God, how I'd like to take it," Sancho mused, "or at least trade it for my own, for it's by far the better mount. The laws of chivalry are really very strict if they don't let you trade one donkey for another. Do you think I could at least exchange their trappings?"

"That I'm not as sure about," said Don Quixote. "But since I have my doubts, you may go ahead, provided it's a real emergency."

"Indeed it is," Sancho replied. "I couldn't need them more if they were for myself."

And he proceeded to adorn his ass with the steed's finery, which greatly enhanced its appearance.

After that, they lunched on the rich leftovers from the day before, when Sancho had emptied the pack-mule's saddlebag, and quenched their thirst in the brook beside their feet. Then, their anger and anxiety now a thing of the past, they set out again in the spirit of knight errantry, not choosing any particular route, but letting Rocinante lead the way.

"I know you want me to be quiet," said Sancho Panza as they rode along, "but there's something I need to tell you before it gets too late. It's on the tip of my tongue."

"Very well," said Don Quixote, "but keep it brief. The longer you go on, the less you make your point."

"For several days now," Sancho said, "I've been thinking how little it avails us to roam these lonely byways in search of adventure when there's not a soul to see or hear us. With all due respect, sir, it seems to me we'd be better off hiring ourselves out to some emperor or prince, in whose service you could perform the selfsame deeds to better profit. Such a lord would be bound to reward us, and there would surely be someone to record Your Worship's feats in writing, to be remembered for all time to come. I say nothing of my own, since they must remain squarely within squirely bounds; but if chivalry permits the feats of squires to be recorded, I have a hunch that mine won't be left out."

"Well put, Sancho," Don Quixote replied. "But before he can serve another, a knight errant has to wander the earth, pursuing adventures where he will. Think of it as a kind of test. Later, once he's proven himself, he can present himself at the court of a great monarch."

Just then, Don Quixote happened to look up. Coming toward them on the road, he saw a row of prisoners fastened head to head, like beads strung on an iron chain.

"Those are galley slaves," said Sancho, "men pressed into service by the king."

"What do you mean, 'pressed into service'?"

"What I mean," said Sancho, "is that they are criminals who have been sentenced to forced labor in the royal galleys."

"However you put it, you're still saying that they're being taken somewhere against their will."

"Indeed I am," said Sancho.

"In that case," replied his master, "I am obliged to act, for my mission is to undo wrongs and assist the wretched of the earth."

"Justice, Your Worship," Sancho said, "which is the very king himself, is hardly committing a wrong against these men, but simply punishing them as they deserve."

By this point the chain of prisoners was upon them. Addressing himself to their guards, Don Quixote asked why they were shackled together in such a fashion. One of the guards replied that they were royal galley slaves on their way to jail. There was nothing more to be said, he added, nor was it anybody's business.

"Be that as it may," said Don Quixote, "I would like to hear directly from each man the reason for his misfortune."

"We have written documents on each of them," said another of the guards, "but Your Worship is welcome to speak with them directly. These rascals don't just like committing crimes, they like to boast about them afterward."

Don Quixote approached the first man in the chain, who replied that he was there for love.

"For love?" asked Don Quixote. "If love can land a man in jail, I should long since have been a prisoner myself."

"It's not what you think," replied the prisoner, a young man some twenty-four years old. "In my case, I fell so deeply in love with a certain basket of fine linen that only the full force of the law was able to pry it from my grasp. I was caught red-handed.

My trial was short. I received a hundred lashes and three years in the galleys."

Don Quixote turned to the second prisoner, who was too forlorn and sad to answer. "This man," the first prisoner explained, "is here for being a canary. In other words, a musician and a singer."

"How's that?" asked Don Quixote. "Being a musician or a singer can put you in the galleys?"

"Yes, sir," the first prisoner replied. "There's nothing worse than singing out of pain."

"But people say that song takes pain away."

"Here it's just the opposite, Your Worship. He who sings a single time weeps forever after."

"I don't understand," said Don Quixote.

"You see, sir," one of the guards explained, "when these people speak of 'singing out of pain,' they're talking about someone who confesses under torture. When this sinner was put to the rack he confessed to cattle rustling. The reason he's so sad is that the rest of these hoodlums make constant fun of him for not holding his tongue."

Now Don Quixote turned to the third man in the chain. "I was short ten ducats," the man replied when he was asked the same question as the others.

"I'd gladly give you twenty," said Don Quixote, "if it would free you from this nightmare."

"If only I'd had them when I needed them," the galley slave replied, "I could have greased the judge's hand and bought my way out of this mess. Today I'd be back in the main square of Toledo instead of being dragged along this highway like a dog. But God is great and patience is its own reward."

Fourth on the chain was a man of venerable appearance, with a long white beard that flowed below his waist. Like the second, he began to weep when Don Quixote asked why he was there, but the next man down lent him his tongue. The old man had run a brothel, he explained, and had also been branded as a wizard.

"All I wanted," the old man said, gathering his courage, "was for everybody to be happy. But that hasn't kept me from being sent to a place I don't expect to leave alive, weighed down as I am by age and a bladder that doesn't give me a moment's peace." With that he began to weep again, and Sancho felt so sorry for him that he slipped him a gold coin from inside his shirt.

Behind the rest came a man of about thirty, a rather dashing figure except that one of his eyes was turned slightly toward the other. He was held more securely than his fellows, with a foot chain so long it was coiled around his body and two iron collars on his neck: one to which the fetter was attached, the other linked to an iron bar across his waist, to which his hands were also manacled. When Don Quixote inquired why he was chained in this unusual manner, the guard replied that he had committed more crimes than all the other prisoners combined, and that even now there was no telling when he might escape.

"If you have anything to give us, sir," this prisoner said, "give it to us now, and then good riddance. We've had enough of your prying into other people's lives. As to my own, know that I am Gines de Pasamonte, whose life has been written with these very hands."

"It's true," said one of the guards. "He's written his life story, and told it well to boot. He pawned his book in jail for two hundred gold coins."

"And I intend to redeem it," said Gines.

"Then it's that good?" asked Don Quixote.

"Good enough to stand beside the best books ever written," said Gines.

"What's it called?"

"*The Life of Gines de Pasamonte,*" the author replied.

"And is it done then?"

"How can it be done," replied Gines, "when my life itself is yet unfinished? So far it covers from my birth to the last time I was thrown in jail."

"You were in jail before?"

"Four years I served God and country," Gines replied. "Believe me, I'm well acquainted with the biscuit and the lash. I'm not sorry to be going back, though, because I'll be able to pick up my book where I left off. I still have a lot to say, and there's more free time than you'd expect in Spanish jails. Not that I need much; I already know by heart the rest of what I want to write."

"You seem a clever enough fellow," said Don Quixote.

"And an unlucky one," replied Gines. "Unhappiness always pursues men of talent."

"It pursues thieves," one of the guards remarked.

At this point Don Quixote turned to the entire chain. "My dear brethren," he began, "by your plight I am moved, convinced, nay, even forced to demonstrate the purpose for which Heaven put me on this earth, wherefore I took the solemn oath of chivalry—namely, to defend the weak and succor the oppressed. First, however, since it is the better part of prudence not to seek by foul means that which might be won by fair, I will ask your guards to set you free; failing which, this lance and sword, along with my right arm, will bring about the same result by force."

"Hear, hear!" exclaimed the sergeant. "Who in God's name does he think he is? The king's own galley slaves no less! As if we had the authority to set them free, or he to ask us to! It's time you ran along, Your Worship. And while you're at it, straighten out that shaving basin on your head."

Don Quixote lunged at him so quickly that before the man knew what had hit him he was lying on the ground. The other guards were dumbstruck by this turn of events but quickly rose to the occasion. Seizing their javelins, they turned on Don Quixote, who would surely have been overcome had the galley slaves not managed at that very moment to break their chain and stumble free. In the ensuing confusion, the guards rushed to attack the escapees, and Sancho released Gines de Pasamonte, who leapt from his iron bonds, seized the sergeant's sword and musket, and cleared the field of guards without firing a single shot.

Don Quixote then summoned all the slaves, who were running about excitedly, and bade them leave at once for El Toboso to present themselves before his lady Dulcinea. "Tell her you bring tidings from the Knight of the Sad Countenance. Then recount the story of this great adventure. When you are done, you may go anywhere you please, and may good luck accompany your every step."

But Gines de Pasamonte explained that he and his fellow escapees must immediately disappear into the woods, before they were recaptured by the Holy Brotherhood.

Don Quixote was furious. "Then you shall go alone," he shouted at Gines, "with your tail between your legs and the whole iron chain piled high upon your back!"

Pasamonte winked at his companions. In seconds there was a hail of stones so thick and sudden that Don Quixote was felled before he could spur Rocinante to safety. Sancho hid behind his ass, but in no time at all he too was lying on the ground. One of the other prisoners flung himself on Don Quixote, seized the shaving basin from his head, and proceeded to pound him with it until both Don Quixote and the basin were nearly broken. The other escapees stripped Sancho of his coat and Don Quixote of his jacket and disappeared into the bright blue air.

All that remained were the ass and Rocinante, Sancho and Don Quixote. The ass hung his head and shook his ears, still imagining that stones were flying overhead. Rocinante, also brought down by a stone, lay flat beside his master. Sancho trembled at the thought that the Holy Brotherhood might return for the prisoners, and Don Quixote fumed at being left in such a state by the very men for whom he had done so much.

PART TWO

By nightfall Don Quixote and Sancho Panza had traveled deep into the heart of the Sierra Morena, the mountains that cut Spain in two. But unruly fate, which composes and disposes according to its own strange whims, decreed that Gines de Pasamonte, the famous thief who had escaped his chains thanks to Don Quixote's might and madness, should have sought refuge in those very hills, also hoping to escape the Holy Brotherhood. He happened to arrive at the spot where Sancho and Don Quixote had bedded down for the night, and immediately recognized them just as they were falling asleep. Gines, who was

neither grateful nor up to any good, decided to steal Sancho's ass, which he spirited away while Sancho slept.

Dawn brought joy to the world but grief to Sancho Panza's heart. "Child of my very self," he cried when he awoke to find his beloved burro missing, "my children's helpmate, my wife's delight, bearer of my burdens, and half my livelihood besides!"

Sancho's pitiful lament woke Don Quixote, who consoled him as best he could and promised him three baby donkeys from his stable when they returned home. Sancho dried his tears, stopped his sobbing, and thanked his master profusely. Don Quixote was elated when they resumed their route, cutting deep into the loneliest, most rugged section of the mountains, which seemed to him the perfect setting for his next adventure. But the last thing on Sancho's mind was more adventure. For the moment his only thought was of his belly, which he satisfied from time to time by reaching into the satchel of provisions he was obliged to carry himself, now that his donkey was no more.

While thus engaged, however, he raised his eyes and saw that Don Quixote had come upon some sort of package, which he was trying to spear with his lance. When Sancho drew closer, he saw a leather case, somewhat the worse for wear and tear but still fastened with a chain. It was too heavy for Don Quixote, so he asked Sancho to pick it up and see what it contained. The

leather was so rotted away that he was able to look inside without breaking the chain. There were four cambric shirts, a richly decorated notebook, and a pile of gold coins. "Praise the Lord!" cried Sancho when he caught sight of the treasure. "At last an adventure worth our trouble!" Don Quixote asked to see the notebook, which was filled with love poems copied in an exquisite hand. "Listen to this," he said, beginning to read aloud for Sancho's benefit:

> What turned my joy to pain?
> Disdain.
> What made a fool of me?
> Jealousy.
> What pierced my loving heart?
> A rival's dart.

"This doesn't tell us anything," Don Quixote said, "except that some poor soul must have lost his way in these deserted hills. Judging by his shirts, his handwriting, and his money, he must have been a gentleman, probably a jilted lover, but what he was doing here and why he left these things behind is anybody's guess."

Don Quixote said he would take the notebook and told Sancho he could keep the money for himself. Sancho kissed his master's hands and they resumed their journey, each wondering to himself what sort of madman would have left such riches lying on the ground.

By the next day, after they had gone a goodly way without a word, Sancho was dying to strike up a conversation. He had been hoping Don Quixote would speak first, but he finally screwed up his courage and broke the silence himself.

"Sir Don Quixote," he said, "give me your blessing and let me return to my house, my wife, and my children. If animals could speak, I could at least bare my heart to Rocinante. But if I have to hold my tongue day after day, especially through such forlorn landscapes as this, I'm as good as dead."

Don Quixote told Sancho he was free to speak his mind, but only for as long as they were in the Sierra Morena.

"In that case," Sancho said, "I won't mince words. What is it you really hope to accomplish in this godforsaken place?"

"Haven't I already told you?" Don Quixote replied. "I aim to imitate Amadis and play the desperate, demented lover; or brave Sir Roland, who went mad when he was spurned by his Angelica, ripping trees from the ground, slaughtering sheep, massacring shepherds, burning cottages, and performing a hundred thousand other feats worthy of eternal fame."

"My good sir," said Sancho Panza, "the knights who did such things were sorely provoked. But you? What reason have you for becoming mad? What lady has scorned you? Or what evidence have you uncovered that the lady Dulcinea del Toboso has betrayed you?"

"That's just the point," said Don Quixote, "and therein lies the beauty of my plan. There's no glory to be won by going mad when you are forced to; but when a knight loses his mind for no good reason, thereby giving his lady an idea what he would do if he had cause—now that's another matter. So, my friend, don't waste your breath trying to convince me to give up my strange, wondrous, thoroughly unprecedented ways. I am mad, and mad

I shall remain until you return with the reply to a letter I intend to send my lady Dulcinea in your hands. If her answer be favorable, I shall be put right in my senses; if it be otherwise, I shall take leave of them for good, in which case I shall be rid forever of my grief, for I'll no longer know one feeling from another. By the way, dear Sancho, have you been taking proper care of Mambrino's helmet? I saw you pick it up from the ground when that ungrateful wretch tried to demolish it."

"Good God, Sir Knight of the Sad Countenance!" said Sancho. "Sometimes I can't believe the things you say. What is one to think when you call a barber's basin Mambrino's helmet? That you must be cracked in the head—that's what. It makes

me think that everything you say about chivalry and winning kingdoms and empires and giving me an island of my own is nothing but hot air. A hoax, in other words. For your information, I have the basin in my bag, all dented, and I plan to trim my beard with it when I get home, if by the grace of God I'm ever reunited with my wife and children."

"Really, Sancho," said Don Quixote, "don't you understand by now that everything to do with chivalry appears to be a dream? Not because it is, but because the hidden enchanters who dwell among us keep changing all our deeds into their opposites. That's why the helmet of Mambrino looks like an ordinary shaving basin to you and everybody else, so nobody will steal it. If people knew what it was really worth, that fellow wouldn't have battered it the way he did and left it lying on the ground. Leave it in your bag, my friend; I have no need of it for now. If I'm to follow in the footsteps of Sir Roland, I must first remove my armor, strip naked as the day I came into this world, and carry out my penance."

At this point in their conversation they arrived at the foot of a sheer rock that jutted up alone against the sky. A gentle stream ran through the lush green meadow where they stood, and many trees and flowers adorned the spot. It was here that the Knight of the Sad Countenance decided to stop and do his penance.

"This is the place I have chosen to bemoan my luck," said Don Quixote, raising his voice. "Oh, Dulcinea del Toboso, day of my night, joy of my grief, guide of my every step, lodestar of my fate! Behold the state to which your absence has reduced me, and reward my faithfulness as you see fit! Oh, solitary trees, my only companions from this day on! Show me by the gentle swaying of your boughs that my presence here does not offend you! And you, my squire, blithe companion of my deeds, commit to memory what you are about to witness, that you may faithfully recount it to my lady."

So speaking, Don Quixote leapt from Rocinante's back, stripped him of both bridle and saddle, and slapped him on the rump. "One yet a captive sets you free," he told the horse. "Go where you will, for on your forehead it is written that you are fleeter than the hippogriff of old."

"Truth to tell, Sir Knight of the Sad Countenance," said Sancho Panza, "if my departure and your madness are in earnest, it would be best to saddle Rocinante up again. Because if I have to walk, God only knows how long it will take me to reach El Toboso."

"Whatever you say, Sancho," Don Quixote replied. "But

you shall not leave for three days' time. First I want you to witness all the things I plan to do and say in my lady's name, so you can give her a complete account."

"What more is there for me to see besides what I've already seen?" asked Sancho Panza.

"I still have to shred my clothes, scatter my arms, dash my head against the rocks, as well as perform several other tricks that will astonish and amaze you," Don Quixote replied.

"For the love of God!" cried Sancho. "You might hit such a pointy rock that the first blow will put an end to your whole penance. Since this is all in good fun anyway, just a jest or joke or spoof, if you have to bang your head, it seems to me it might as well be on something soft like cotton—even water. I'll still tell your lady that you rammed your head against a rock as hard as any diamond."

"Thanks all the same, but I'll have you know this is no laughing matter but the solemn truth; otherwise, I'd be breaking the law of chivalry, which forbids us to lie. The blows to my head must be real and they must hurt, with no ifs, ands, or buts."

"Very well then," Sancho said, "but please—write your letter and let me be off to El Toboso. I'll tell your lady such wonderful things about you that she'll turn soft as a glove, even if she's tough as a chestnut to begin with. Then I'll fly through the air like a wizard and bring you her honey-toned reply."

"But how shall we write the letter?" asked the Knight of the Sad Countenance. "Ah, I know. I'll write it in my notebook, and when you come to a village with a schoolmaster you can have it copied out on proper paper or give it to a parish clerk to be transcribed."

"What about the signature?"

"It can be signed 'Yours till death, the Knight of the Sad Countenance,'" said Don Quixote. "It doesn't matter if the handwriting is different. Dulcinea can't read or write, and she's never seen my handwriting before, so she won't notice. I should

tell you that in all the twelve long years I've loved her I haven't seen her more than a few times, and our love has never gone beyond a modest glance, because her father, Lorenzo Corchuelo, and her mother, Aldonza Nogales, keep such a strict and careful eye on her."

"Do you mean to tell me," Sancho began, "that the daughter of Lorenzo Corchuelo is Lady Dulcinea del Toboso, otherwise known as Aldonza Lorenzo?"

"I do indeed," said Don Quixote.

"As I live and breathe," said Sancho Panza. "I know her well, and I can tell you she's built like an ox, if not like a whole stable. Yes, she's a strapping thing, all right. She can wield an ax as well as any man. What muscles, what lungs! And a real mouth on her too. Of course she must have changed a lot since I last saw her, because the sun and wind play havoc with a woman's looks when she stays out in the fields day after day. Well, well, well. And here I was believing that your Dulcinea was a princess or at least a person of some stature. When you come right down to it, what good would it do Lady Aldonza Lorenzo, I mean Lady Dulcinea del Toboso, if all the knights in the world came courting her on bended knee? She'd probably die laughing."

"I've told you before," said Don Quixote, "and I'll tell you again. Sometimes your mouth is too big for your own good. I happen to be perfectly content to imagine and believe that Aldonza Lorenzo is the greatest princess in the world. In case you didn't know, two qualities inspire love more than all others: beauty and reputation. These my lady Dulcinea has in abundance. In beauty she has no rival and in reputation few can touch her."

"What I meant to say, sir, is that Your Worship's always right and I'm a fool. Give me the letter and I'll be on my way."

Don Quixote took out his notebook and calmly began to write. When he was done, he read it aloud so Sancho would remember what it said, just in case anything should happen to it on the way.

DON QUIXOTE'S LETTER TO
DULCINEA DEL TOBOSO

Sovereign and noble lady:

He who has been pierced by the lance of
absence and wounded in the very fabric
of his heart, sweet Dulcinea del Toboso,
wishes you the health he cannot claim for
himself. If thy beauty spurns me,
if thy strength be not with me but
against me, ill shall I yet bear my grief,
which is not only great, but everlasting.
My good squire Sancho will give you all the
details. Ungrateful beauty and beloved foe!
Inasmuch as I remain at thy beck and call,
I am all thine should you wish to succor me;
if not, do as you wish, and by ending
my life I will satisfy both thy cruelty and
my desire.

Thine until death,
The Knight of the Sad Countenance.

"By my father!" Sancho said when he had finished. "That's the noblest thing I ever heard! You say exactly what you mean, and the Knight of the Sad Countenance is the perfect signature. I swear there's nothing you don't know."

"In my line of work," said Don Quixote, "you have to know everything."

"I'm off to saddle Rocinante," Sancho said. "I'm not going to wait around to watch your penance. I'll tell Lady Dulcinea what you want me to, and she'll be more than satisfied."

"At least stay to see me naked. I'll run through the first dozen or two tricks in less than half an hour. After that, I don't mind if you make up the rest."

"For God's sake, Your Worship, I couldn't bear to see you naked. It would only make me cry, and after all the tears I shed last night for my beloved donkey, I'm in no condition for fresh grief."

"Very well, then. I'll wait for you right here," said Don Quixote. "Still, just to be on the safe side, cut some broom sprigs and scatter them from time to time along your route. They'll lead you back to me like the thread in Theseus's labyrinth."

"I'll do as you say," said Sancho Panza.

Then, with many tears on both sides and not before Don Quixote had given him his blessing, Sancho climbed into Rocinante's saddle and set out for El Toboso, stopping every now and then to scatter the sprigs of broom as he had promised.

But he had gone only a hundred yards when he turned back. "On second thought, Your Worship, you were right," he said. "If I'm to swear that I saw you perform certain tricks, I ought to witness at least one, though I've already seen the biggest one of all: your refusal to budge from this godawful place."

"Just you wait," said Don Quixote. "I'll be done in nothing flat."

Quickly pulling down his breeches, he stood barebottomed, wearing just his shirt. Then, with no further ado, he leapt up twice, clicked his heels in the air, and did two somersaults,

exposing certain parts of himself, which sent Sancho scurrying back to Rocinante, ready and able to swear that his master was mad as a hatter.

After traveling all day along the road to El Toboso, Sancho came to the same inn where he had suffered his mishap with the blanket. Once again he felt as if he were flying through the air, which left him reluctant to go past the door, even though it had been ages since he'd had a decent meal.

He was still hesitating when two men came out into the courtyard.

"Tell me, Sir Priest," one said to the other, "isn't that our good neighbor Sancho Panza, who left town as Don Quixote's squire?"

"Indeed it is," replied the priest, "and that is Don Quixote's horse."

As chance would have it, it was the priest and barber from his village, the same men who had burned Don Quixote's books. They were eager for news of Don Quixote, but Sancho decided not to tell them where he was or what he was up to at that moment. So when they asked after his master he replied that Don Quixote was extremely busy with a matter of great importance, the nature of which he could not reveal for all the tea in China.

"Oh no you don't, Sancho Panza," said the barber. "If you don't tell us where he is, we'll have no choice but to conclude that you've robbed and slain him. After all, you're riding his horse."

"You have no right to threaten me like that," said Sancho Panza. "Let each man die according to his fate or by the will of God who made him. If you really want to know, my master's up on that mountain over there, having the time of his life doing a penance."

And out poured the story of all the adventures that had befallen him and Don Quixote and the letter he was carrying to Lady Dulcinea del Toboso, who was the daughter of Lorenzo Corchuelo, with whom Don Quixote was head over heels in love. The priest and the barber were amazed, even though they already knew that Don Quixote had lost his mind. They asked to see the letter, and Sancho Panza told them it was written in a little notebook, and that Don Quixote had asked that a proper copy be drawn up at the first opportunity. The priest offered to transcribe it himself in his best hand, but when Sancho felt inside his vest there was nothing there.

The notebook had remained behind with Don Quixote, and Sancho had forgotten to ask for it before he left.

Sancho turned pale as death. Once again he patted himself all over, only to realize afresh that he could not produce the letter. He immediately slapped himself a dozen times and began to pluck his beard out hair by hair until his face and chin were bloody.

At this terrible sight the priest and the barber asked what

could possibly have happened to make Sancho treat himself so badly.

"I've lost the notebook," Sancho said, "and that's not all." He told them that his beloved burro had been stolen, and the priest consoled him by offering to help him draw up a promissory note for the three baby donkeys Don Quixote had promised him on their return. With that Sancho was comforted and offered to recite the letter to Dulcinea, which he said he knew almost by heart.

"Tell it to us then," the barber said, "and we'll transcribe it for you later."

Standing first on one foot and then on the other, Sancho scratched his head and tried to summon up the letter. He looked down at the ground and up at the sky, and then he looked back at the ground. Finally, after a long silence, he began to speak.

"Hang it all, Sir Priest, I'll be damned if I remember. All I know is that it started out with 'Noble and slovenly lady.'"

"'Slovenly' doesn't sound right," said the barber. "Could it have been 'sovereign'?"

"Yes, that's it," said Sancho. "And then, if memory serves me right, it continued with 'He that is pierced, sleepless, and wounded kisses your hands, ungrateful and thankless beauty.' After that there was something about the health and sickness that he wished her, and then it ran on until he signed it 'Yours until death, the Knight of the Sad Countenance.'"

The pair were not a little amused by Sancho's memory. They begged him to repeat the letter so they could learn it by heart themselves and later write it down. Sancho recited it three times again, and three times over he made three thousand comical mistakes. Then he explained that if he received a favorable response from Lady Dulcinea del Toboso, Don Quixote was going to try to become an emperor, or at any rate a monarch. By that point, Sancho said, he himself would surely be a widower and would marry one of the empress's ladies-in-waiting, the heiress to a large estate, after which he would have nothing more to do with isles or inlands, thank you all the same.

So seriously did Sancho Panza recount all this, wiping his nose from time to time, that the priest and the barber were freshly astounded by the strength of Don Quixote's madness, which had spirited his poor squire's brains away along with his own. But they were loath to dispel Sancho's illusions; besides, they found his chatter quite amusing.

"What we have to do now," remarked the priest, "is figure out a way to free your master from the senseless penance he's performing. And if we want to think well, we had better go inside and eat."

Sancho agreed but said he would wait for them outside; he promised to tell them later why he didn't want to go indoors. The priest and the barber disappeared into the inn, and a little later the barber brought him some dinner, along with fodder for Rocinante. Soon afterward the priest came out and explained the course of action he and the barber had concocted. The priest would dress up as a damsel in distress, and the barber would pretend to be her squire. In this disguise they would go to Don Quixote and beg a boon of him, which Don Quixote, as a good knight errant, could not refuse. The favor was that he follow the damsel wherever she might lead and that he undo a grievous wrong a wicked knight had done her. She would also beg him not to remove her mask or inquire about her rank until he had finished punishing the knight.

The priest was sure Don Quixote would agree, and that they would be able to lure him from the mountains and lead him home, where they would try to find a cure for his strange madness.

The priest's plan did not displease the barber—just the opposite, in fact—and they began to prepare themselves at once. The priest asked the innkeeper's wife to lend him a dress, and the barber asked for an oxtail from which he could fashion a long beard. When she asked what they planned to do with these strange articles of clothing, they told her about Don Quixote

and how he had lost his mind and was holed up in the mountains whence, thus disguised, they hoped to lure him home. From their description, the innkeeper and his wife immediately recognized their erstwhile guest, the madman whose squire had been so rudely blanketed. In the end the landlady outfitted the curate to perfection. She gave him a wool dress stiffened with black velvet stripes and a bodice of green velvet with white satin piping. He tied a piece of sheer black taffeta across his forehead and another one over his beard. Then he put on his broad hat, wrapped his cloak around him, and mounted his mule sideways like a woman, while the barber mounted his, his new beard falling to his waist.

But no sooner had they left the inn than the priest had second thoughts: it was unseemly, he realized, for a clergyman to go about in such attire, so he asked the barber to trade clothes with him. If the barber refused, he would go no further, and to hell with Don Quixote.

When Sancho caught up with them he could not help laughing at their costumes. The barber finally agreed to play the damsel in distress, but insisted on wearing his own clothes until they reached their destination. So he folded up his dress and the priest packed up his beard, and they rode on. Meanwhile, Sancho continued to recount the adventures that had befallen him and Don Quixote in the Sierra Morena, but with one exception. He said nothing about the leather case and all it held.

The next day they came upon the trail of broom sprigs Sancho had left to mark the path to the spot where he had left his master. It was time, he told his two companions, to put on their disguises. It had already been agreed that Sancho would not give them away. And if Don Quixote were to ask him, as he certainly would, whether he had delivered the letter to Dulcinea, he must say yes, but that since she could neither read nor write she had replied by word of mouth, commanding him to come to her at once on pain of losing her affection.

Sancho proposed that he should ride ahead and give Don Quixote Dulcinea's reply, since that alone might do the trick without putting them to any trouble. The priest and the barber agreed and sat down to wait beside a gentle stream in the cool shade of the towering rocks and trees. It was three o'clock in the afternoon of a hot August day, which made their refuge all the more inviting.

As they were relaxing in the shade, they chanced to hear a voice of surpassing sweetness.

> What turned my joy to pain?
> Disdain.
> What made a fool of me?
> Jealousy.
> What pierced my loving heart?
> A rival's dart.

The song gave way to a deep sigh. The priest and the barber waited a moment and then got up to see who could possibly have such a beautiful voice and such a broken heart. They had not gone far when, rounding the corner of a rock, they saw a young man dressed all in rags. At first he remained silent, his head bent forward. But after the priest implored him, he addressed them with the following words.

"Whoever you may be, I see that you are messengers from Heaven. But before you attempt to draw me away to a better place, first listen to my tale, for once you have heard my countless woes you may wish to spare yourselves the effort of consoling one whose heart is broken past repair."

They begged him to proceed, and with their encouragement the sad-faced youth began his tale.

"My name is Cardenio; my birthplace one of the finest cities of Andalusia; my family rich; and my misfortunes so great that all my parents could do for me was weep, for earthly riches are powerless against fate's heavy hand. In our city there dwelled a maiden as noble and rich as I, whom I loved from my tenderest years, as she loved me. As we grew older our love grew too, until one day I decided to ask her father for her hand. He told me my own father should come see him.

"But when I entered my father's chamber, he was holding a letter from Duke Ricardo, a Spanish grandee whose estate lies in the richest part of Andalusia, who had summoned me to serve his eldest son and promised to find me suitable employment afterward. I was stunned by the letter, but even more so by my father's words. I was to leave the following morning, he said, and should give thanks to God for leading me toward the future I so richly deserved.

"I told my Lucinda what had happened and begged her father to give me a few days until I figured out the duke's intentions.

"I was well received by the duke's household, but by none as well as by his second-born son Fernando, a lively, likable fellow who quickly became my friend and who told me of a love affair that was causing him no little grief. He was enamored of a farmer's daughter, a girl so beautiful, so modest, and so well-mannered that he had offered to marry her in hopes of winning her affection. But now he was having second thoughts. He proposed that we spend a few months at my father's, during which he hoped to forget her. He would tell the duke we were going to my native city to buy horses, since the best horses in the world are bred there.

"The duke gave his permission, and we traveled to my city. As soon as we arrived I went to see Lucinda. To my undoing, I told Fernando of my passion, praising her beauty, her grace, and her wit, and arousing in him a great desire to see her. Finally I let him join me one evening beneath the window where it was my wont to talk with my betrothed. Lucinda was dressed in a loose shift, and looked so beautiful in the candlelight that Don Fernando instantly lost both his tongue and mind; in other words, he fell madly, hopelessly, in love.

"To make a long story short, Fernando sent me to his elder brother on the pretext of borrowing some money to pay for six horses we had bought while in my city. The brother bade me wait eight days, even though he was a wealthy man and could easily have given me the sum I asked for right away. But several days after I arrived, a man handed me a letter from Lucinda explaining that Don Fernando had asked to marry her and that her father had agreed. The wedding was scheduled to take place in utmost haste and secrecy, two days from when she wrote.

"The sudden rage I felt toward Don Fernando, along with my fear of losing the prize I had earned through so many years of service and devotion, lent wings to my feet, and by the following morning I was standing at Lucinda's door.

"'Cardenio,'" she said, "'today I am to be a bride. At this very moment the traitor Fernando and my greedy father are waiting in the hall; however, they shall witness not my wedding but my death. I want you to be present at this sacrifice. There is a dagger in my dress, with which I intend to end my life and show you the great love I've borne you all along and bear you still.'

"Here the night of my sadness fell; the sun of my happiness set; I was left without light in my eyes or sense in my head. My feet were rooted to the ground, and I was unable to move. But when I realized how important it was that I be present for what might happen, I forced myself to enter the house. I found a hiding place in the great hall itself from which I could see everything without being seen.

"Fernando arrived dressed in his ordinary clothes. A few minutes later Lucinda appeared with her mother and two maids, adorned as befit both her beauty and her station, the very image of courtly fashion and delight.

"After they were all assembled, the local priest came in and took them each by the hand. When he said, 'Do you, Lucinda, take Don Fernando to be your lawful husband?' I stuck my head out from behind the tapestries to be sure I heard Lucinda's reply. Just when I thought she was going to draw her dagger, I heard her say in weak and fainting tones, 'I do.' Don Fernando said the same two words and placed a ring on her finger. But as he turned to kiss her, she fainted dead away into her mother's arms.

"Everyone was in an uproar, and when her mother unlaced Lucinda's dress to give her air, she found a letter which Don Fernando immediately snatched and read by the light of the torches. When he had finished, he sat down in a chair and put his hand on his cheek, lost in thought and paying no attention to the attempts being made to bring his bride back from her swoon. At this point I ventured out and returned to the house where I had left my mule. Then, like Lot, I left my city without looking back. I rode all night, and at dawn I struck into these mountains, where I wandered for three days without seeing a soul. Finally I asked some herdsmen where the wildest portion of the mountain lay, and they showed me this spot.

"My usual dwelling is a hollow cork tree. The shepherds who ply these hills feed me out of charity. And so I shall spend what remains of my wretched life, until the day Heaven decides to bring it to a close."

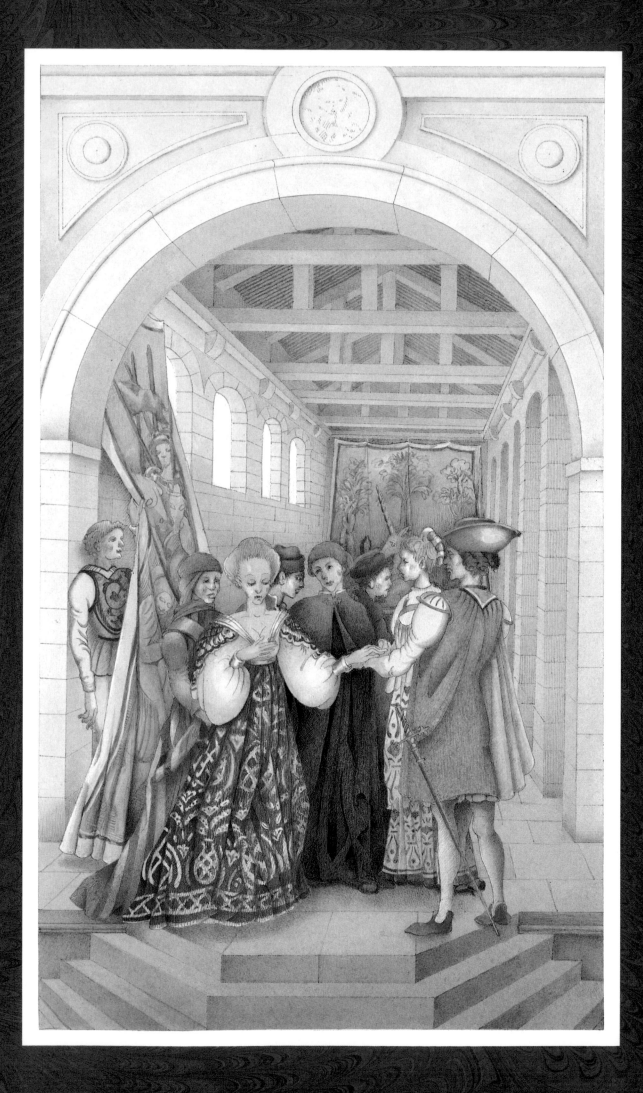

Here Cardenio ended his sad tale. But just as the priest was preparing to offer him some words of consolation, they heard another mournful voice, whose story will be told in the next chapter.

Once again the priest and his companions got up to look for the source of the voice that had reached their ears. They had not gone twenty yards when, coming around a jutting boulder, they saw a young man seated underneath a tree. He was dressed like a peasant, in a short gray cape, a cap of the same color, matching breeches, and a pair of leggings that were rolled halfway up his calves, which were as white as marble. They were unable to see his face because he was bent over a small brook in which he was washing his feet. In fact, he was so absorbed in his ablutions that he did not hear them approach. They were astounded at the beauty and delicacy of his feet, which looked like two pieces of pure crystal and seemed ill-suited to trudging up and down the fields behind an oxen team and plow. When he had finished he looked up, revealing a face so piercingly beautiful that Cardenio whispered to the priest that it must be a god.

Then, still unaware of their presence, the youth took off his cap and, shaking his head from side to side, let fall a headful of gold hair as splendid as the sun. With this the priest and his companions realized that their young man was a woman, and one more beautiful than any they had ever seen—all of them, that is, except Cardenio, who later said he could only compare her to Lucinda.

Moved by admiration and the desire to know who she might be, the three men stepped forward from their hiding place. At this the woman jumped to her feet and, without putting on her shoes or tying her hair, bolted away in fright. But she had gone only a few steps when the sharp stones pierced her feet and she fell down.

"Stop, lady, whoever you are," the priest called out. "There is no need for you to flee."

Then, helping her up by the hand, he continued, "What your clothes deny, your hair reveals. If we cannot relieve your anguish, we can at least advise you. So, dear lady, or dear sir—whichever you prefer—banish the fear our presence here has caused you and tell us your story, whether it be good or bad."

The disguised maid stood spellbound as he spoke, staring at the three of them without a word, but she soon gave a deep sigh and broke her silence.

"Since this lonely peak cannot conceal me, nor my long hair allow my tongue to lie, I may as well comply with your request, though I fear the tale of my misfortune will cause you grief as well as pity."

After putting on her shoes and tying up her hair, she sat down on a stone. The three men gathered around her and she began her tale, doing her best to hold back the tears that sprang to her eyes.

"Here in Andalusia there is a duke who has two sons. The elder one is heir to his estate and upright character, the younger to I know not what, unless it be to treason and deceit. My parents are tenants of this lord, but though of humble birth, they are quite rich.

"They are farmers, simple folk whose wealth and generosity of spirit have gradually transformed them into gentry, even aristocrats of sorts. But their greatest wealth and nobility lay in me, their only child. I was the apple of their eye and the staff of their old age; my every wish was their command. Whenever I went out, I was so closely veiled and guarded that my eyes scarcely saw any more of the earth than my feet touched. Even so, the eyes of love, or should I say the eyes of greed, found me out in the person of Fernando, the younger son of the duke I mentioned earlier."

At the mention of Fernando's name Cardenio turned pale and broke into a sweat. The priest and barber were afraid he was about to have a fit, but he stood stock-still, staring at the farmer's daughter and trying to imagine who on earth she could possibly be. She, however, unaware of his reactions, continued her tale.

"I won't tell you all the tricks Fernando had up his sleeve. He bribed the servants in our house and lavished gifts on all my relatives. Our street became a carnival, with musicians keeping everyone awake night after night. And who could possibly keep track of all the love letters he sent? Of course, with my parents' advice, I resisted; given the difference between our ranks, I knew that his campaign was for his own amusement, not for any benefit it might bring me.

"One day Fernando found out that my parents were planning to seek a suitable match for me. That night I was all alone in my room with my serving maid when he suddenly appeared before me. He grabbed me in his arms, and I was unable to defend myself.

"Inexperienced as I was and confused by his tears and sighs, I came to believe the lies he whispered in my ear. 'Were it not for my honor,' I told him, 'I would give you what you wish, for though a humble farmer's daughter, I count myself as noble as yourself. Still, only a lawful husband can win from me what you desire.'

"'If that is all that worries you, lovely Dorotea,' the traitor said, 'I hereby give you my hand.'"

When Cardenio heard the name Dorotea, his suspicions were confirmed, but he still said nothing, not wanting to interrupt the story whose ending he had all but guessed.

"Then," continued Dorotea, "he took one of the holy images I kept in my room and held it up while giving me his solemn oath that he would be my husband. I begged him to think twice about it, because his father would be furious if he married a peasant girl like me, one of his own tenants. But all my protests were in vain.

"I told myself that I would hardly be the first to rise from low to high estate through marriage, just as Fernando was not the first inclined by beauty or blind love—probably the latter—to marry beneath his station. And so, persuaded as much by my own arguments as by his oaths and charm and tears, I finally accepted his desire as my own.

"But morning could not come fast enough for Don Fernando, who rushed outside before the sun was up, escorted by my maid. I told him he was welcome in my chamber any time he pleased, until such time as our marriage was made public, for I now belonged to him. He returned the following night, but never again.

"I combed the streets for weeks until I tired of looking. Finally I heard the news. Fernando had married a beautiful young woman from a nearby city. Her name was Lucinda, her family was noble, and strange tales were being told about their wedding."

When Cardenio heard the name Lucinda, he only shrugged his shoulders, bit his lips, and frowned. Then his eyes became a flood of tears. But Dorotea continued with her story, unperturbed.

"I was so angry that at first I wanted to tell the world how Fernando had betrayed me. But that very night I came up with a plan. I borrowed the clothes I have on now from a shepherd in my father's employ. I stuffed some clothing of my own into a pillowcase, along with some money and some jewels, just to be on the safe side. Then, without telling my treacherous maid, I slipped from my house under cover of darkness, accompanied only by this shepherd and my worst fears.

"We traveled more than two days before reaching the city where Lucinda's parents lived. The first man I stopped told me more than I wanted to hear. He showed me the house and told me that on the night of the wedding, after Lucinda had said yes, she had fallen into a deep faint, and that when her husband loosed her dress to help her breathe, he had found a letter written in Lucinda's hand in which she declared that she could not become his wife because she was already married to Cardenio, a noble gentleman of the same city. She had agreed to the wedding only so as not to disobey her parents. And that's not all:

after trying to stab her with the dagger he found hidden in her dress while she was still unconscious, Don Fernando escaped. Lucinda did not recover from her swoon until the following day, when she told her parents that she was really and truly the wife of this Cardenio. And there was more: Cardenio, people said, had been present at the wedding but had rushed from the city in despair when he saw her married to Fernando, leaving behind a letter declaring his intention to flee to where nobody would ever find him. All this was common knowledge in the city. Indeed, people spoke of nothing else, especially when they learned that Lucinda had vanished from her house and that her parents were beside themselves with grief.

"This news gave me some hope. Perhaps Heaven had prevented Don Fernando from taking a second wife so he would recognize his duty to his first.

"I was still there in the city, turning these thoughts over in my mind, when I heard a town crier announce that a handsome sum would be paid to anyone who found me, with a detailed description of my person, down to the very clothing I had on. I immediately made my way into these mountains. How many months I spent alone here I don't know, but at long last I found a herdsman who took me as his servant. I've been his farmhand ever since, always managing to stay out in the fields so that my hair would not give me away, as it has finally done to you.

"This, gentlemen, is the true story of my tragedy; judge for yourselves whether the sighs you overheard, the words I have just spoken, and the tears I shed were justified or not."

With this she fell silent, and her face turned a color that revealed the depth of her shame and sorrow. Her listeners too were overcome, feeling both pity and wonder at her disgrace. Then, just as the priest was about to offer her some words of consolation and advice, Cardenio stepped forward. "Does this mean you are fair Dorotea, the only daughter of rich Clenardo?"

Dorotea was astonished to hear her father's name, especially on the lips of one so lowborn as the man in rags who had addressed her.

"Who are you, friend, who knows my father's name?"

"I," replied Cardenio, "am that unlucky man Lucinda called her husband. I am none other than Cardenio, reduced to this desperate, ill-clad, incoherent state by the very hand that brought you to your current straits. Yes, Dorotea, I was present at the scene of Fernando's crime, and yes, I couldn't bear to see what happened after my Lucinda fainted, and I rushed headlong from her home. But if your tale be true, as I believe it is, perhaps Heaven has reserved a happier ending for us both than we dared hope. For if Lucinda cannot marry Don Fernando, since she is mine, nor Don Fernando marry her, since he is yours, then we may yet believe that each will be restored to rightful each, since all four of us are still alive."

Dorotea was so overwhelmed by Cardenio's speech that she tried to kiss his feet in gratitude. But Cardenio would not allow her. The priest spoke for both of them, seconding Cardenio's hopes but urging the two of them to accompany him to his village, where he would outfit them with everything they might require. Once there, they could decide whether to go looking for Fernando or return Dorotea to her parents. Cardenio and Dorotea thanked him and agreed to go along.

Just then they heard shouts which they recognized as Sancho Panza's. He had found Don Quixote, naked as the day he came into this world except for his shirt, and nearly faint with hunger, sighing for his Dulcinea. Sancho had told him of Dulcinea's command, but Don Quixote refused to leave his hiding place before he had done more deeds worthy of her favor. If this kept up, said Sancho, Don Quixote might never become an emperor, and he would never get his isle. They must therefore think of some new plan for getting him home.

The priest told Cardenio and Dorotea the ruse they had

devised, and Dorotea immediately pointed out that she could play the damsel in distress better than the barber. Not only did she have the perfect dress, but she knew exactly how to speak because, she said, she had read many books of chivalry.

"In that case," said the priest, "let's get to work at once."

Dorotea opened her pillowcase and extracted a costume of the finest cambric, with a green shawl made from some other splendid cloth. Then she took a necklace and assorted jewels from a wooden chest, and in a flash she had transformed herself into the image of a rich and high-placed lady. Everyone was charmed by her grace, her beauty, and her noble mien, but no one was as dazed as Sancho Panza, who swore he had never seen so beautiful a creature in his whole life—which was the truth. He asked the priest to tell him who this lovely lady was and what on earth she was doing in such an out-of-the-way place.

"This beautiful lady," the priest replied, "is none other than the heiress to the kingdom of Micomicon. Such is your master's fame that she has traveled all the way from Guinea to seek a boon of him—namely, that he right a wrong inflicted on her by a wicked giant."

"Happy the search and happy the find!" Sancho exclaimed. "But please, Sir Priest, convince my master to marry this lady forthwith, so he'll come quickly to his empire, and I to my heart's desire. It all depends on his marrying this princess—I don't know her title yet, so I can't call her by her proper name."

"Her name," replied the curate, "is Princess Micomicona, which is what you would expect. After all, she's the sovereign of Micomicon."

"But of course," said Sancho Panza. "I've known many men who took their names and titles from where they lived—Pedro of Alcala, Juan of Obeda, Diego of Valladolid. It stands to reason that they follow the same custom in Guinea, and that the queens there are named after their kingdoms."

By this point Dorotea had mounted the priest's mule and the barber had glued his phony beard back on his chin. They asked Sancho to lead them to his master, reminding him not to let on that he knew either the curate or the barber.

They had gone about a mile when they caught sight of Don Quixote in a clearing full of rocks, fully clothed now but without his armor. Dorotea urged on her palfrey, with the oxtailed barber following behind. When they arrived, the "squire" leapt from his mule and reached up to take Dorotea in his arms. She dismounted with great ease and fell to her knees at Don Quixote's feet.

"I will not rise, oh valorous, distinguished knight, until Your Grace grants me a boon that will raise your honor and prestige in the name of the most grievously aggrieved and wrongfully wronged maid the sun has ever shone on."

"I will not answer you, beauteous lady," Don Quixote said, "nor hear another word about your plight, until you rise from this position."

"I will not rise, sir," replied the damsel in distress, "until you grant me what I wish."

"I grant it freely," Don Quixote said, "so long as it in no wise hurts or harms my obligations to my king, my country, and the lady who holds sway over my heart."

"Your Worship can easily grant the boon she asks," Sancho whispered in his master's ear. "All you have to do is slay a giant. The lady is Her Highness the princess Micomicona, queen of the great Ethiopian kingdom of Micomicon."

"I repeat that I grant your request," said Don Quixote. "With the help of God and my right arm, you shall soon find yourself restored to your ancient throne."

Then he asked Sancho to prepare Rocinante and help him on with the assorted pieces of his armor, which hung like trophies from the branches of a nearby tree.

The barber was on bended knee, trying with all his might to keep from laughing and not to lose his beard, which would have brought everybody's hopes to naught. But as soon as he heard Don Quixote's promise, he jumped to his feet and helped the so-called princess mount her mule. Then he climbed onto his own, and Don Quixote mounted Rocinante, leaving Sancho to go on foot. Sancho missed his beloved ass, but he was of good cheer, for it seemed to him that his master was finally on his way toward becoming an emperor. He had not the slightest doubt that Don Quixote would marry the princess and at the very least become king of Micomicon.

Meanwhile, Cardenio and the priest, who were still hiding behind some bushes, were at their wits' ends for an excuse to join the others. But the priest, whose imagination served him well, soon hatched a plan. Taking out a pair of scissors from their leather case, he snipped off Cardenio's beard and dressed him in his own gray jacket and black cape. Cardenio looked so different that he would not have recognized himself if he had looked into a mirror. The rest of the party had already set out while the two of them were changing, but they ran ahead and managed to be standing on the plain when Don Quixote and his traveling companions emerged from the pass.

The priest stared at Don Quixote as if he were struggling to recognize him. He stood there for a goodly while and then ran up to him with open arms.

"Welcome, Mirror of Chivalry!" he cried. "My countryman Don Quixote de la Mancha, protector and comforter of those in need! The flower and cream of all nobility, and very quintessence of knight errantry!"

As he spoke, he clasped Don Quixote's left knee. Don Quixote looked him up and down, and when he finally recognized him he was astonished.

"Please, Sir Curate," Don Quixote said, "it isn't right that I should go on horseback while so reverend a person as yourself travels on foot."

"I am but a humble priest," the priest replied, "and will gladly ride one of the mules, if nobody objects."

"I'm sure my lady the princess will be pleased to ask her squire to give you the saddle of his mule. He can ride on the crupper if the animal will have it."

"Certainly," replied the barber. And he jumped to the ground, offering his saddle to the priest, who accepted in a trice. But just as the barber was climbing up behind him, the mule reared up and gave two mighty kicks that would have sent the

barber reeling had they struck him in the head or chest. As it was, the barber fell to the ground in fright, forgetting all about his beard, which came unstuck. He promptly clasped both hands to his face and began to moan that his jaw was broken.

"Behold a miracle!" Don Quixote exclaimed when he saw the beard on the ground without a trace of blood. "His beard has fallen from his face as clean as if it had been shaved."

The priest, thinking on his feet, ran up to the beard and carried it to where the barber lay moaning on the ground. Mumbling some words under his breath, he clasped the barber's head close to his chest and pressed the wayward beard back on, explaining that this was a special charm for restoring beards. When he stepped back, there was the barber, as fully bearded and healthy as before. Don Quixote was awestruck and begged the priest to teach him the spell when he had time. Since it had worked a complete cure, it must, he thought, be good for more than beards.

"Indeed it is," replied the priest, promising to teach it to him at the first opportunity.

As they prepared to go on, they all agreed that the priest should ride in front and that the others should take turns along the way until they reached the inn. With three of them in the saddle—that is to say, Don Quixote, the princess, and the priest—and three on foot—Cardenio, the barber, and Sancho Panza—Don Quixote turned to address the princess.

"Lead on, Your Highness, wherever you please."

But before she could reply, the priest spoke up. "Whither will Your Ladyship convey us? Toward Micomicon, perchance?"

Dorotea was quickwitted enough to understand that she was expected to say yes.

"Yes," she said, "that's exactly what I had in mind."

"In that case," said the priest, "we shall have to pass right through my village. From there Your Highness can travel directly to the coast, whence you can set sail for Micomicon."

"What I'd like to know," said Don Quixote as they prepared to leave, "is what has brought my friend the curate to these parts, why he's all alone, and how he can be so thinly clad."

"The answer to that, Your Worship," replied the curate, "is simple. You see, our good friend the barber and I were traveling to Seville to collect some money that a distant relative of mine had sent from the New World, some sixty thousand silver ducats in all—hardly a trifling sum, you will agree. But yesterday, just as we were riding down this very road, four thieves appeared out of the blue and robbed us blind. They even took our beards and left us in such dreadful shape that the poor barber had to find a false one. As to this young lad," he added, pointing toward Cardenio, "why, he's unrecognizable! The strangest part of all is that everyone for miles around says the men who jumped us were all galley slaves. Rumor has it they were freed not far from here by a man who was either clear out of his mind or else as great a rogue as they. He set a pack of wolves loose among sheep, a swarm of flies loose over honey. In other words, to make a long story short, he thumbed his nose at justice, disobeyed his king and rightful lord, and committed a deed through which his soul is lost and his body will gain absolutely nothing."

Sancho had told the barber and the priest the adventure of the galley slaves, which is why the priest laid it on so thick as he retold it, eager to observe Don Quixote's every reaction. The knight changed color with each word and dared not admit that he had been the one who set the four thugs free.

"Well," the priest said in conclusion, "may God in His mercy forgive the man who spared those criminals the punishment they so deserve."

"By my faith, Sir Priest," Sancho exclaimed, "it was my master who performed that feat. And not because I didn't warn him. I knew it was a sin to set them free."

"You numskull!" shouted Don Quixote. "A knight errant doesn't stop to wonder whether the oppressed and downtrodden he helps are paying for something they did or didn't do; he looks to their suffering, not their sins. Anyone who disagrees with that is a liar and an ignoramus. But this trusty sword will set him straight, so help me God."

And as he spoke he drew himself up tall in his stirrups and pulled his visor down over his forehead.

Dorotea realized that everyone but Sancho Panza was making fun of Don Quixote. "Sir Knight," she said, eager to join the merriment, "see that you don't forget the boon Your Worship granted me. No other adventure, no matter how pressing, should take precedence over the task you promised me."

"I shall be still, my lady," replied Don Quixote, "and restrain the anger that has justly risen in my heart. But in exchange for my good will, I beg you to reveal the nature of your troubles, as well as on whom, and why, and on how many I am to take due, complete, and satisfactory revenge."

"I shall be glad to," Dorotea replied, settling comfortably into her saddle and clearing her throat as she prepared to tell her tale. Cardenio and the barber moved closer so they could hear what sort of story she would manage to concoct, and so did Sancho Panza, who had fallen for her ruse as completely as his master.

"First of all, gentlemen, you should know that I go by the name of . . ." and here she stopped, because she had forgotten the name the priest had given her.

Luckily, the priest was quick to the rescue. "It's no surprise, Your Highness," he said, "that you should be confused. Misfortune often has that effect, and those who have suffered some reverse of fortune often lose their memory or even forget their names, as has just happened to Your Exalted Self, the princess Micomicona, lawful heiress to the great kingdom of Micomicon. Now, with this reminder, Your Highness should be able to continue with your tale."

"Indeed," replied the damsel. "As I was saying, then, my father the king, Tinacrio the Wise, was very skilled in magic. He foresaw that my mother, Queen Jaramilla, would die before him and that he himself would follow suit soon after, leaving me an orphan. Still, all this upset him far less than the fact that an enormous giant, lord of a large island just a stone's throw from our kingdom, whose name was Pandafilando the Scowler (because although his eyes are perfectly well-placed, he continually squints as if his eyes were crossed, not because he has trouble seeing but in order to strike fear and dread into the hearts of everyone he meets)—this terrible giant, according to my father, would invade the kingdom as soon as I was orphaned. My only escape would be to marry him; but my father knew that I would never think of doing that—or of marrying any other giant, for that matter. He advised me not to remain in the kingdom after he died and not to resist Pandafilando's invasion, but to leave immediately for Spain, where I would enlist the help of a famous knight whose name, I believe, was Don Azote—or Don Gigote."

"Don Quixote, he must have said," said Sancho Panza.

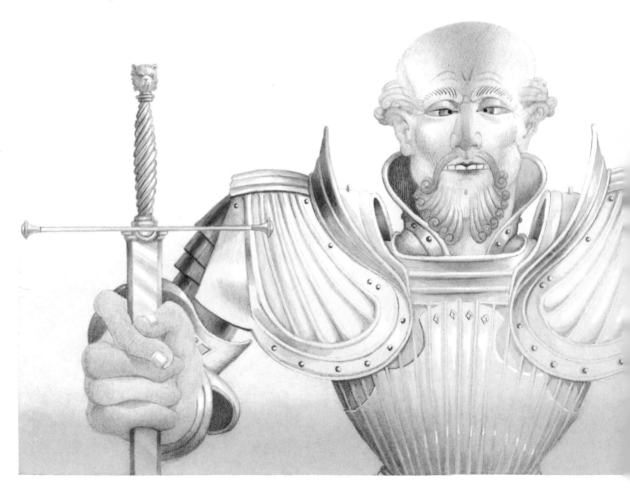

"Otherwise known as the Knight of the Sad Countenance."

"That's it," said Dorotea. "He also said that he would be a tall, gaunt-faced man, with a small dark mole on the right side of his body, just beneath his left shoulder, or somewhere like that, with little hairs sticking out of it like bristles on a brush."

At this, Don Quixote began to remove his shirt.

"Why should Your Worship want to get undressed?" asked Dorotea.

"To see if I have the mole your father described," said Don Quixote.

"There's no need for you to go to such extremes, Your Worship," Sancho said. "I already know you have a mole exactly like the one Her Highness has described. It's on your back."

"What difference does it make exactly where it is?" said Dorotea. "We're among friends, so there's no need to bother with such trifling details. You have a mole, and a mole is a mole. I know that my father was right in everything he saw, and that

I am equally right in entrusting my fate to Don Quixote. I can tell by his face that he's the knight my father meant. As soon as our ship landed in Osuna, I heard tell of all his exploits, and my heart immediately told me that he was the man I sought."

"Osuna?" said Don Quixote. "Osuna, my dear lady, is not a port."

But before Dorotea could reply, the priest stepped into the breach. "I'm sure Her Highness meant that after her ship landed in Malaga, the first place she heard about Your Worship was Osuna."

"That's exactly what I meant," said Dorotea.

"Well, then," said the priest. "Will Your Majesty continue?"

"There's nothing more to say," said Dorotea, "except that fate has smiled on me by leading me to Don Quixote, thanks to whom I once again feel like the mistress and ruler of my realm. He's promised to accompany me wherever I lead, which of course will be directly to Pandafilando the Scowler, so that he may slay him right away and restore what the giant has usurped. All this will come to pass exactly as my darling father, Tinacrio the Wise, predicted. My father also left a message in some foreign alphabet (Chaldean or Greek, I think, but I can't read it) to the effect that if this knight, once he has beheaded the evil giant, should wish to marry me, I should consent to be his lawful wife and grant him possession of my kingdom."

"Did you hear that, Sancho?" said Don Quixote. "Tell me we don't have a kingdom to our name, and a queen to boot!"

"I swear we do!" cried Sancho Panza, and at that he gave two pirouettes and leapt into the air with sheer delight. Then, seizing the bridle of Dorotea's mule, he fell on his knees before her and begged her to let him kiss her hands, to show the world that he took her as his lady and his queen.

Who among that company could keep from laughing at the madness of the master and the gullibility of his squire? Dorotea held out her hands to Sancho Panza and promised to make him

a great lord of her realm as soon as she was reinstated on her throne. And Sancho thanked her with words that once again brought laughter to the lips of all those present.

Meanwhile, the priest took Dorotea aside and congratulated her on her story, praising both its cleverness and its concision, as well as its close resemblance to tales of chivalry. Dorotea said that she had often whiled away her time with suchlike reading but that she didn't have the faintest idea about the different ports and provinces of Spain, which was why she had made the mistake about Osuna.

"I realized that," the curate said. "That's why I interrupted you and set things straight. Still, isn't it amazing how readily this gentleman believes our most elaborate lies, just because they're dressed up in the style of the books that he's so fond of reading?"

"Indeed it is," said Cardenio. "In fact, it's so unheard of that I wonder whether anyone who tried to invent a character like him would have the genius to pull it off."

While this discussion was taking place, Sancho noticed a gypsy riding toward them on an ass. When the man drew closer he saw that it was Gines de Pasamonte, disguised as a gypsy so nobody would know him. Putting two and two together, he realized he was looking at his own beloved ass. "Gines, you thief!" he cried. "Give me back my ass, the apple of my eye! Give back what isn't yours, you bastard!"

But all his curses were unnecessary. At the very first shout, Gines jumped from the ass and disappeared into thin air. Sancho ran up to his burro and threw his arms around him. "How have you been, my love, my sweet?" he murmured, caressing his mount as if it were a person. "My darling, my treasure, companion of my every step!" Everyone congratulated him on recovering his ass, especially Don Quixote, who promised all the same to make good on his offer of three baby donkeys, for which Sancho Panza was most grateful.

"And now," said Don Quixote, "it's time to find the giant. I'll slice off his head and restore the princess to her throne, and then I'll return to see my Dulcinea. I'll give her such a wonderful explanation that she'll be grateful for my long delay, since my deeds only increase her fame and glory. For everything I have accomplished, am accomplishing, and shall accomplish in this life I owe to her good will and the fact that I belong to her, body and soul."

"You really are stark raving mad, Your Worship, aren't you?" exclaimed Sancho Panza. "Do you mean to tell me that you plan to travel all that way for nothing and let a princely marriage slip right through your fingers? You should be ashamed of yourself. Why, I've heard that Micomicon is bigger than Spain and Portugal combined. Forgive me, but I'm old enough to give you advice. A bird in the hand is worth two in the bush. If you lose an opportunity like this, you'll have only your own self to blame."

"Listen, Sancho," Don Quixote replied, "if the reason you're advising me to marry is so I can be king after I kill Pandafilando and therefore reward you as I've promised, there's no need to worry: I can give you what you wish without marrying the princess. All I have to do is insist that if I slay the giant, I receive part of the kingdom and that I'm free to bestow it on anyone I wish. And whom else would I give it to but you?"

"In that case," Sancho said, "choose a piece along the coast, so that if I'm not entirely happy there I can take the first ship home. Meanwhile, don't go see the lady Dulcinea. First find the giant and get it over with; for God knows it will bring us great honor and profit."

"You're right," said Don Quixote, and vowed not to visit Dulcinea until he had restored the princess to her throne.

Finally, with no further adventures or untoward events, they resumed their journey and arrived at the inn that was the dread and terror of Sancho Panza. This time, like it or not, he would have to go inside.

When the innkeeper, his wife, their daughter, and Maritornes saw Don Quixote approach, they came running out to welcome him and all his party. But he returned their greeting with restraint and asked them to prepare a better bed than the one they had given him the time before. The innkeeper's wife replied that she would make him a bed fit for a prince so long as he was prepared to pay more than the first time around. Don Quixote said he would, and she set him up in the attic where he had slept before. He went straight to bed, since he was badly rattled and his mind was not all there.

Moments later, Sancho came hurtling from the loft. "Come quick!" he shouted at the top of his lungs. "My master's locked in the grisliest battle I've ever seen. He sliced that giant's head off at the neck as if it were a turnip!"

"Have you taken leave of your senses, Sancho?" asked the priest. "The giant lives six thousand miles from here!"

Suddenly they heard a great tumult from upstairs. "Halt, thief!" came Don Quixote's voice. "Stop where you are! I've got you now, you lousy cur! Your scimitar is worthless now!"

It sounded as if he were slashing at the walls.

"Don't just stand there!" Sancho said. "Go upstairs and try to break up the fight or at least help my master, even though he probably doesn't need it anymore. The giant is probably as dead as dust and already giving God a full account of his rotten ways and evil life. I saw it with my own two eyes. There was blood all over the floor and a huge head lying on its side, bigger than a wineskin."

"As I live and breathe!" exclaimed the innkeeper. "That Don Quixote has probably run his sword through the wineskins that were hanging at the foot of his bed. And what this poor devil thought was blood is probably red wine."

With that he ran up to the attic, and all the others after him, where they found Don Quixote in the strangest getup in the world. He was dressed only in his shirt, which wasn't long enough in front to cover his thighs and was six inches shorter in the back. His legs were long and skinny and not terribly clean, and on his head he wore a small red cap that belonged to the innkeeper. He had draped a blanket over his left arm, and in his right hand he held his sword, with which he continually stabbed the air, spinning around every which way in the room and shouting strange words as if he were actually fighting a giant. The best part of all was that his eyes were closed, because he was sound asleep and dreaming. So vivid was his image of the adventure that lay ahead of him that in his dream he had already reached Micomicon and was fighting the terrible giant to the death.

He had slashed the wineskins back and forth, and the whole room was full of wine. The innkeeper was so upset at this sight that he immediately fell on Don Quixote and began to pummel him with his fists; if not for Cardenio and the priest, who stepped between them, he would have brought the war with the giant to a precipitous end. Despite all this, the wretched knight did not wake up until the barber brought a pitcher of cold water from the well and poured it over him. Even then he did not come fully to his senses. He seemed not to have the foggiest idea of who or where he was or what he had been doing.

Meanwhile, Sancho was down on all fours looking for the giant's head, which of course was nowhere to be found. "I'm convinced that this whole house is under a spell," he said. "Last time we were here I hardly slept a wink. And now I can't find the head I saw sliced off with my own eyes. I saw blood gushing from the body like a fountain."

"You crazy infidel!" exlaimed the innkeeper. "Don't you realize that what you call blood and a fountain are these wineskins full of holes and this sea of spilled red wine? May the soul of the man who did this swim in hell!"

"All I know," said Sancho Panza, "is that if I don't find that head, my countship will melt away like salt in water."

Sancho awake was worse than his master asleep: his master's promises had given him a one-track mind.

The innkeeper was in despair at the squire's nonchalance and the havoc his master had wreaked on his guest room. He swore that this time around they would not get away without paying their bill.

The priest was holding Don Quixote by the hands when the knight suddenly fell to his knees, believing that he had finished his adventure and was now in the presence of the princess Micomicona. "Exalted and most famous lady," he proclaimed, "Your Highness may now rest assured that this vile monster will not harm you, and so may I, who hereby count myself released from the pledge I gave you."

"Wasn't that just what I said?" said Sancho Panza. "You see? I wasn't drunk after all. The giant is dead, and my countship is in the bag!"

Who could help but laugh at the nonsense of these two, master and servant? Everyone was laughing except the innkeeper, who kept mentioning the Devil. Finally, and not without a lot of trouble, the barber, the priest, and Cardenio managed to steer

Don Quixote back to bed, where he fell sound asleep. Then they went out to the courtyard to comfort Sancho Panza for not having found the giant's head. They had a harder time calming down the innkeeper, who was fit to be tied at the sudden death of his wineskins. His wife too was storming up and down, cursing the day the knight errant blew into her house. "May God put a bad end to his adventures and to all knights errant in the world!" she shouted. "He won't get away with it, I tell you! Not if I can help it!"

All this and more the innkeeper's wife poured out in a great frenzy, seconded by her loyal servant Maritornes, while her daughter looked on with a smile.

The priest promised to compensate them for the wine and the torn wineskins. And Dorotea consoled Sancho Panza by promising to give him the best countship in her kingdom once she had made sure that the giant was really and truly dead. Sancho was much pleased by this and assured the princess that he had seen the giant's head, which she would recognize by its long beard. If it did not turn up, he said, it was because the whole inn was under a spell. Dorotea said that she believed him and that he had no need to worry because everything would turn out to his heart's content.

Just then the innkeeper, who was standing in the doorway, announced the approach of a new group of guests.

"Who are they?" asked Cardenio.

"Four men on horseback," the innkeeper replied, "two on foot, and a woman dressed in white from head to toe. She has a veil over her face and she's seated on a wooden saddle."

"Are they near?" the priest inquired.

"If they were any closer, they'd already be inside."

At this, Dorotea covered her face and Cardenio slipped into Don Quixote's room, only moments before the new arrivals rode through the gate. Still in their black riding masks, the men helped the veiled woman from her horse and settled her onto a chair just outside the room where Cardenio was hiding. As she sank into the chair, she let out a deep sigh and her arms fell to her lap, as if she were about to faint.

"What ails thee, lady?" Dorotea asked, going up to where the woman sat. "If it be anything that lies within a woman's powers to remedy, I will gladly help you."

"Don't waste your breath," said one of the masked horsemen. "Madam is ungrateful by her very nature. And don't encourage her to speak unless you are prepared to hear the lies that flow unbidden from her mouth."

"I've never lied," the lady said, breaking her silence. "Just the opposite, in fact. Truthfulness alone has brought me to this wretched plight."

Cardenio, separated from her only by the door, could hardly believe his ears. "Good God!" he cried. "What's this I hear? Whose lovely voice has reached my ear?"

At this the lady turned around and, seeing no one behind her, stood to go into the room. But the masked gentleman barred her way. As they struggled, her veil fell off, revealing a face of incomparable beauty. The gentleman was so intent on keeping his grip that he was unable to hold up his mask, which had slowly begun to slip. When Dorotea caught sight of his face, she saw that he was Don Fernando, her long-lost husband, at which she gave a high-pitched moan and pitched backward in a faint, which would certainly have killed her, had the barber not been standing there with open arms to break her fall.

Meanwhile, the priest came running up to throw water on Dorotea's face. When he lifted her veil, Don Fernando was almost struck dead by the sight. But this did not loosen his hold on the woman who was struggling to free herself from his embrace, who had recognized Cardenio by his cries. Cardenio had also heard Dorotea's moan and, thinking that it was Lucinda, came running from the room where he was hiding. The first person he saw was Don Fernando, with his arms around Lucinda. Don Fernando immediately recognized Cardenio, and they all stood rooted to the floor, barely understanding what had happened. Dorotea stared at Don Fernando, Don Fernando at Cardenio, Cardenio at Lucinda, and Lucinda at Cardenio.

The first to break the silence was Lucinda.

"Just think," she said, turning to Don Fernando, "how Heaven, moving in mysterious ways, has brought me back to my true husband."

Dorotea, meanwhile, recovered from her swoon. Now it was her turn to speak.

"I, my lord," she said, throwing herself at Don Fernando's feet, "am that humble country girl, the hapless Dorotea, whom you once wanted for your wife. Perhaps my untarnished love for you can make up for the beauty and nobility of the lady you hold in your arms. You cannot be the fair Lucinda's, because you are mine, nor can she be yours, because she is Cardenio's."

Poor Dorotea went on and on, speaking with such feeling and weeping so profusely that even the other men in Don Fernando's party were moved to tears. Lucinda felt a mixture of pity and admiration; but much as she wanted to whisper some words of comfort in her ear, Don Fernando still held her tight.

At this point Fernando's friends, along with the priest and the barber, who had witnessed the whole scene, implored him to be moved by Dorotea's tears. Not by chance, they said, but by Heaven's express will, had everyone been reunited in this unlikely spot. Besides, only death could part Lucinda and Cardenio. If Don Fernando would turn his eyes to Dorotea, he would see that few or none could equal her, much less excel her.

To these arguments the priest added so many others that Don Fernando's valiant heart finally softened. As a sign that he had given up and accepted the priest's good advice, he bent down and took Dorotea in his arms.

"Rise, my lady," he said. "The woman I hold in my heart must not kneel at my feet. All I ask is that you not reproach me for my misconduct and neglect. I wish Lucinda a long and happy

life with her Cardenio, and may Heaven grant me the same with you."

With these words he embraced Dorotea again and pressed her cheek to his own so tenderly that he had all he could do to keep from weeping. But Lucinda, Cardenio, and almost everybody else showed no such restraint. Their tears flowed so abundantly, some for their own happiness and some for others', that anyone arriving on the scene would have thought some terrible disaster had befallen them. Even Sancho wept, although he later said it was because he had just learned that Dorotea was not the princess Micomicona, from whom he expected such great gifts, and because his hopes of winning an isle were going up in smoke.

Dorotea wondered whether her new happiness was just a dream. Cardenio had similar doubts, and so did Lucinda. Don Fernando gave thanks to Heaven for having freed him from the intricate labyrinth in which he had come within a hair's breadth of losing not only his honor but his soul. Everyone at the inn rejoiced at the happy resolution of such a difficult and complicated story. The priest dotted all the i's and crossed the t's, congratulating each of the four lovers in turn. But the most jubilant of all was the innkeeper's wife, because Cardenio and the priest had promised to make up for all the damage she had suffered on account of Don Quixote.

Sancho Panza, the very picture of despair, went to see his master, who was just waking up. "Sleep on, Sir Knight of the Sad Countenance," he said. "You can stop worrying about slaying giants or restoring the princess to her throne. It's all over and done."

"I believe you," said Don Quixote. "The battle I fought with that giant was the fiercest I ever hope to see. So much blood poured out of him it flooded the whole floor!"

"More like wine, Your Worship, don't you think?" said Sancho Panza. "You may not have noticed yet, but I'll have you know that your dead giant is a sword-slashed wineskin; his blood the twelve gallons of red wine it contained; and his severed head—oh, the hell with it—and may the Devil take it all!"

"I beg your pardon?" replied Don Quixote.

"You have only to get up," said Sancho, "and you'll see what a fine mess you've made. And you'll see the queen become an ordinary lady by the name of Dorotea, along with a whole host of other things that will startle and amaze you."

"They will do nothing of the sort," said Don Quixote. "I told you the last time we were here: everything that happens in this place is the result of magic."

Sancho handed him his clothes, and while he was getting dressed the priest told Don Fernando and the others about Don Quixote's madness and the plan they had come up with to entice him home. He also told them almost all the stories he had heard from Sancho Panza, which drew oohs and ahs from their lips, not to mention laughter, and they agreed that this was far and away the strangest form of madness a madman could devise. That wasn't all: since the happy resolution of Dorotea's woes had put an end to their cherished scheme, they would have to come up with another way of luring Don Quixote home.

Just then Don Quixote entered the room, decked out in his entire collection of accouterments, including the somewhat battered helmet of Mambrino. Don Fernando and his companions were flabbergasted by his strange appearance, especially his long, sallow face, his jumble of assorted weapons, and his solemn bearing. They waited silently to see what he would say, and he soon obliged them, addressing the beautiful Dorotea in his gravest tone of voice.

"My faithful squire informs me that Your Highness has been brought low and your very self destroyed. If this was by order of that necromancing wizard, your late father, he didn't and still doesn't know the half of what he should. If he had read his chivalry, he would have realized that lesser knights than I have overcome obstacles far greater."

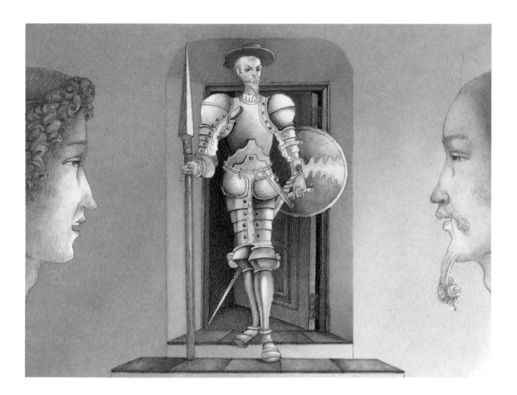

Here Don Quixote stopped to await the princess's reply. But she, knowing that Fernando planned to continue the deception until they had successfully returned Don Quixote to his village, replied with great aplomb.

"Whoever told you, brave Knight of the Sad Countenance, that I've been changed or altered told you wrong, for I'm the same today as I was yesterday. The truth of the matter is that my luck has turned, bringing about certain changes, as it has granted me my heart's desire, but none of that has altered me from who I was before nor in any wise transmuted my desire to avail myself of your valorous, invincible, and invulnerable right arm. Indeed, had it not been for you, good sir, I believe I should never have known the stroke of great good luck that has so recently come my way, of which I can imagine no better witness than the present company, who can testify to the truth of what I say. All that remains is for us to set out first thing tomorrow morning, since today is almost gone. Our further success I leave to God and your brave heart."

When Dorotea had finished speaking, Don Quixote turned to Sancho Panza. "You, my little squirrel of a Sancho, are the

meanest rogue in Spain. Didn't you just tell me that this princess had become an ordinary maid named Dorotea and that the head I sliced from that dreadful giant should go to hell, along with a whole pack of other lies that made me more confused than I've ever been in my whole life? I swear to God"—and here he gritted his teeth and his gaze swept Heavenward—"I have a mind to wreak such vengeance on you as will turn the brains of every lying squire in the world to mush!"

"Whoa!" said Sancho Panza. "I may have been mistaken regarding the transformation of Her Highness the princess Micomicon, but in the matter of the giant's head, the slashing of the wineskins, and the spilled red wine, I am not wrong, so help me God. Those skins lie slashed at the foot of the very bed in which you were resting, and the wine has turned your room into a lake."

"Forgive me, Sancho Panza," said Don Quixote, "but you are stark raving mad. Enough is enough."

"Indeed it is," Don Fernando said. "Since Her Highness bids us to set out tomorrow, let us do as she suggests and spend tonight in pleasant conversation. Tomorrow we shall all accompany

Sir Don Quixote, for we are as eager as anyone to observe the splendid and unusual feats he will assuredly perform in the course of the great task in which he is engaged."

Meanwhile, the Devil, who never sleeps, ordained that the barber from whom Don Quixote had stolen Mambrino's helmet arrived at the inn. When he caught sight of Sancho Panza and Don Quixote, he raised a great hue and cry, accusing Don Quixote of stealing his shaving basin out from under his arm. Unbeknownst to Don Quixote, the priest, eager to avoid further disputes, paid the barber eight gold coins, and the barber wrote him a receipt in which he declared the matter of the basin paid in full and promised not to bring further charges either now or evermore.

After observing this exchange, the innkeeper demanded that Don Quixote settle his account. He swore that neither Rocinante nor Sancho Panza's ass would leave the inn until he had been paid to the last cent. All this the priest amicably resolved, and Don Fernando paid the bill.

With all pending matters settled, Don Quixote decided it was time to resume his journey and complete the great adventure to which he had been called. His mind made up, he knelt before Dorotea, who refused to let him speak until he rose, a request with which he obediently complied.

"Most beauteous lady," he said, getting to his feet, "for all we know, your enemy the giant may at this very moment be building insurmountable fortifications that will prove impervious to my untiring arm. So, my lady, let us not tarry, but depart while our luck holds."

"I thank you, Sir Knight," the princess replied, imitating Don Quixote's refined and lordly style. "May Heaven grant both our desires, for indeed I have no other wish than thine. Let us, as you say, depart forthwith."

"By God," said Don Quixote, "when a lady puts her fate in my hands, I can't resist the chance to raise her up again and restore her to her rightful throne. Sancho, saddle Rocinante, harness your ass, and prepare the queen's horse. Let us be off."

But what with one thing and another, a whole day came and went before everyone was ready. In the meantime, the priest and the barber concocted a new plan for luring Don Quixote home and curing him of his peculiar madness.

First, they hired a wagoner who happened down the road with a yoke of oxen. Second, they built a sort of cage from crisscrossed poles, which was large enough for Don Quixote to ride in comfortably. Third, the priest instructed Don Fernando and his party, along with the innkeeper and his whole family, to cover their faces and dress up in various disguises.

Next they crept into the room where Don Quixote was sleeping off the turmoil of the previous days. They tiptoed up to where he lay, oblivious of their designs, and tied him hand and foot, so that when he awoke he could only stare in wonder at the crowd of unfamiliar faces. His lively imagination immediately went to work. He was convinced they were ghostly figures from the enchanted castle, which he took as proof that he was now under a spell. Which was exactly what the priest had hoped and expected him to think.

Of all those present, only Sancho was undisguised, but although he was close to sharing the same illness as his master, he did not fail to recognize the others. Still, he kept his mouth shut, afraid to speak until he saw where his master's abduction was leading. Don Quixote too said not a word, also waiting to learn more about the shape of his misfortune.

They dragged the cage into his room, placed him inside it, and nailed it shut with crosspieces of wood so that it wouldn't spring open at the first bump in the road. But before they could leave the room they heard a frightful voice, as terrifying as the barber could make it (not the barber of the shaving basin but the one from Don Quixote's village).

"Oh, Knight of the Sad Countenance!" he cried. "Be not aggrieved by the jail in which you find yourself conveyed, thanks to which you shall more quickly complete the great adventure on which you have so valiantly embarked. For when the wild lion of La Mancha has joined the white dove of El Toboso and the yoke of matrimony has settled over them, there will issue forth the valiant whelps who will follow in the mighty pawsteps of their father. As to you, most noble and obedient squire, be not disturbed to see the flower of knight errantry borne away before your eyes. For you shall soon be raised and exalted to such heights that you shall not recognize yourself, and your master's promises shall be manifoldly manifested and fulfilled."

Toward the end of this prophecy, the barber raised his voice to such a pitch and then lowered it so tenderly that even those in on the joke nearly believed they were hearing the truth.

Don Quixote was comforted by the barber's words, whose meaning he immediately grasped. For he understood that he would soon be married to his beloved Dulcinea del Toboso, from whose happy womb would spring the little lion cubs, his sons, to the great and everlasting glory of La Mancha.

"Whoever you may be," he sighed, "who have foretold such great good fortune, let me not perish before I see your joyful promises fulfilled. As to my squire Sancho Panza, I trust in his good heart and conduct and know that he will not abandon me, for better or worse. For whatever shall come to pass, even if I am unable to give him the island I have promised, he shall at least receive his wages. I have made provision for them in my last will and testament, which is already signed and sealed."

Sancho Panza bowed his head with great restraint and kissed both of Don Quixote's hands. He couldn't kiss them separately, for they were tightly bound.

Then the apparitions hoisted the cage onto their shoulders and placed it on the oxcart. Before it could move off, the innkeeper's wife, her daughter, and Maritornes came out to say goodbye, pretending to weep at Don Quixote's disgrace.

"Weep not, good ladies," he consoled them, "for mishaps such as this are part and parcel of the profession I profess; indeed, if such calamities did not befall me, I should hardly count myself a true knight errant. Less famous knights don't suffer as I do, for nobody remembers they exist. Forgive me, ladies, if I have in any way caused you displeasure. And pray God deliver me from these chains, wherein some evil enchanter has contrived to hold me. I shall never forget the favors you have done me in this castle. If I am ever free again, I shall reward them and repay them as they richly deserve."

While the ladies of the castle were occupied with Don Quixote, the priest and the barber took their leave of Don Fernando and his party and of the happy women in their midst, especially Dorotea and Lucinda. Don Fernando gave the priest his address so the priest could send him word of Don Quixote's fate and promised to let the priest know how matters fared on his end, especially Lucinda's return home. They all hugged each other one more time and bade each other one final farewell.

Then the priest and the barber, both wearing their riding masks, mounted their respective mules and set out after the cart.

The order of their procession was as follows: first the cart, driven by its owner; then Sancho Panza on his ass, leading Rocinante by the rein; then the priest and the barber, bringing up the rear. Don Quixote was seated in his cage, hands bound tight and feet straight out, propped against the bars so silently and patiently that he seemed not a man of flesh and blood but a statue made of stone.

Not long after they set out, the priest turned around and noticed six or seven horsemen gaining on them from behind. These travelers, eager to reach a place to stay in time for their siesta, quickly overtook the procession which, being in no particular hurry, was moving at a far more leisurely pace.

When the fast travelers reached the slow ones, they exchanged polite greetings. On seeing Don Quixote in his cage,

one of the riders, no less a personage than a canon of Toledo, could not help but inquire why they were transporting him in such a fashion.

Don Quixote beat the others to a reply. "Are you by any chance," he asked the canon, "acquainted with what we call knight errantry? If so, I shall be glad to tell you the cause of my misfortunes. If not, I need not waste my breath."

At this point the priest and the barber rode forward, hoping to prevent their scheme from being revealed.

"To tell you the truth," the canon said, in response to Don Quixote's question, "I know more about chivalry than I do about philosophy. So, at least in this regard, you are at liberty to tell me what you wish."

"Very well," said Don Quixote. "In that case, good sir, I'll have you know that I was put into this cage by enchanters filled with envy and deceit; for virtue rankles evil spirits more than it finds favor with the good. I am a wandering knight whose name shall be inscribed in the shrine of immortality as an example and legacy to future centuries, that they may know the path to follow should they wish to reach the veritable peak and summitry of chivalry."

"Sir Don Quixote de la Mancha speaks the truth," the priest ventured at this juncture. "He is indeed under a spell, through no fault of his own, but thanks to those who cannot abide virtue and whom bravery offends. This, sir, is the Knight of the Sad Countenance—perhaps you have heard of him before—whose brave deeds and heroic feats shall endure in bronze and marble for all time, despite the ceaseless efforts of those who would erase all traces of his glory."

When the canon heard both the jailed man and his keepers speak in such a manner, he nearly crossed himself in sheer amazement, as did the other members of his party.

Now Sancho Panza, hoping to put the final touches on the sauce, himself addressed the canon. "The truth of the matter, gentlemen, is that my lord Don Quixote de la Mancha is no more under a spell than my mother." Then, turning to the priest, he continued, "Sir Priest! Do you really think I don't know who you are? Or that I don't suspect where these new tricks of yours are heading? Believe me, I've seen through your disguise, and I've already figured out what's up your sleeve. The Devil take your soul! Why, if not for Your Reverence, at this very moment my master would be married to the princess of Micomicon and I would be a count—at least a count, because that's the very least I could expect from my lord the Knight of the Sad Countenance, not to mention the magnificence of my own service. Ah yes, the wheel of fortune spins faster than a millstone, and those who only yesterday were riding high today lie on the floor. Actually, it's my wife and children I feel really sorry for. Because just when they had every right to expect me to come through the door as a governor or viceroy of some island or kingdom, they'll see me turned into an ordinary farmhand. Think twice about the way you're treating my master, Sir Priest. Because you may have to answer the Almighty when you reach the other side. I'm sure He'll want to know why you locked Don Quixote in a cage and kept him from his knightly deeds while he was your captive."

"Hang it all, Sancho!" exclaimed the barber. "Are you cut from the same cloth as your poor master? It won't be long before we'll have to slap you beside him in the cage, for I swear you've already caught some of his humor and chivalry."

In the meantime, the priest invited the canon to ride ahead with him, promising to tell him the mystery of the cage, as well as several other things that would intrigue him. The canon agreed, and he and his servants were amazed to hear the story of the life, madness, and strange ways of Don Quixote.

"To tell you the truth," the canon said when he was done, "these books of so-called chivalry are dangerous to the republic. I must confess that although I have read the beginnings of almost all of them, I have never managed to read a single one of them straight through. The fact of the matter is that they all sound the same. If their primary purpose is to entertain, I don't see how they can hope to attain it when they are so crammed full of grandiose nonsense. If you reply that the men who compose such books write them as fiction and therefore have no obligation to tell the truth, I should reply that the more fiction resembles truth, the better the fiction; the more it is lifelike, the more we like it. Made-up stories have to suit the imagination of their readers and be told in such a manner that, keeping the reader in suspense, they amaze, astound, provoke, and amuse, letting wonder and delight go hand in hand."

The priest listened with great interest, for the canon struck him as a man of considerable understanding. Then he explained that he shared the canon's grudge against books of chivalry and had even gone so far as to burn Don Quixote's entire collection. And he told the story of the inquisition, with the titles of the books he had consigned to the flames as well as those he had spared, which gave the canon a good laugh. Yet for all he had said against them, the canon continued, books of chivalry had one thing in their favor—the chance they offered a good mind to display itself to full advantage. For they provided a broad and spacious field through which the pen could run at will, now describing shipwrecks, storms, and battles; now tragic, regrettable events, now joyful, unexpected ones; here a beautiful lady, and here a gentleman; there a grandiloquent braggart, there a wise and noble prince. The writer could depict the subtlety of Ulysses, the piety of Aeneas, Achilles's valor, Hector's woes—in short, all those attributes that constitute the perfect hero, sometimes bringing them together in a single figure, sometimes parceling them out among several different characters.

"And if all this," the canon concluded, "is done in a pleasant style with an ingenious plot, keeping as close as possible to the truth, the result will be a fabric woven out of various and beautiful threads which when finished will be perfect enough to achieve the stated purpose of such works, which is to delight and instruct at the same time, as I have said."

When the canon and the priest had reached this point in their conversation, the barber caught up with them. "This, Sir Curate, is the place I told you about. Here we can spend a peaceful siesta while our beasts enjoy the pasture."

"It looks fine to me," replied the priest, and the canon, delighted by the lovely valley that stretched before them, decided to stop too. He wanted to continue his conversation with the priest and to hear more about Don Quixote's astounding feats.

While this was going on, Sancho saw his chance to speak with his master without the continual presence of the barber and the priest. He went up to the cage in which Don Quixote was traveling.

"I can't go on, Your Worship," he said, "without telling you the true story of your spell. The men with scarves over their faces are our village priest and barber. I think they've spirited you off like this out of envy because you're way ahead of them in famous deeds. As proof of what I say, I'm going to ask you a question. If you answer as I think you will, you'll put your finger on the trick and see that you're not under a spell at all, but that you've simply gotten muddled."

"Ask what you wish, Sancho my son," Don Quixote replied, "and I will answer you as best I can. But as to your idea that these men who keep running back and forth are our friends and neighbors the barber and the priest, while they may look the same to you, don't believe it for a minute. My enchanters must simply have taken on their likeness, for magicians can assume any identity they wish."

"Holy Mother!" Sancho shouted. "Can you really be so thick between the ears, Your Worship? Don't you see I'm telling you the honest truth, and that there's more malice than enchantment to this imprisonment of yours?"

"Stop your hocus-pocus," said Don Quixote, "and ask your

question. I've already promised you a straightforward reply."

"Very well, Your Worship," Sancho replied. "Without mincing words, and with all due respect, Your Worship, I'd like to know whether, in the time you've been cooped up in this cage—under this spell, as you would have it—whether, sir, in all this time, you've ever had the urge to pass water, as the saying goes?"

"What on earth are you talking about, Sancho? What do you mean by 'passing water'?"

"Is it possible Your Worship doesn't understand what every schoolboy knows?" Sancho replied. "What I want to know, Your Worship, is whether you've felt the need to do what no one else can do for you?"

"Ah—now I understand! Of course I have. In fact I feel it right this minute. Help me, for things are not as clean in here as they could be!"

"I'll do everything I can," Sancho replied. "You see, if you could ride Rocinante again, we might pick up where we left off with our adventures. If not, we can always return to the cage where, as your faithful squire, I promise to shut myself up along with Your Worship if you should be too weak, or I too dumb, to carry out my plan."

Sancho begged the priest to release his master from the cage for a short while; otherwise, his cell would not be as clean as befit a knight of Don Quixote's stature. The priest agreed, so long as he had some assurance that Sir Don Quixote would not disappear for good.

Sancho gave his word, and the canon echoed him, so long as Don Quixote himself agreed not to leave them without first asking permission.

"I agree," said Don Quixote, who had been listening all along. In fact, he added, if they didn't let him out, it would not be long before he began to offend their noses, unless they planned to keep a certain distance from his cart.

The canon took him by the hands, which were still tied, and they led him from the cage, which made him infinitely happy. The first thing he did was stretch his whole body. Then he went up to Rocinante and slapped him on the haunches. "Flower and mirror of all horses," he exclaimed, "with God's will we two shall once again meet in the image of our hearts' desire: you with your master on your back, and I astride you, performing the mission for which God brought me to this world."

Having said this, Don Quixote went off into the woods with Sancho Panza. When he returned he was greatly relieved and more eager than ever to put his squire's plan into execution.

The canon stared at him, marveling at the curious form his madness took and by the seeming coherence of everything he said; for the knight only lost his stirrups, as the saying goes, when the conversation turned to chivalry. And so, after they had all sat down to await their midday meal, which was being brought from a nearby inn, the canon, moved by compassion, addressed himself again to Don Quixote.

"Can the harsh and idle reading of books of chivalry, good sir, really have affected your wits to such a point that you believe yourself to be under a spell, and other similar things which are

as far from the truth as any outright lie? How can any human mind possibly believe in the multitude of knights you've named, not to mention all those steeds, spells, damsels, giants, princesses, skirmishes, dragons, disguises, and every other sundry absurdity that books of chivalry contain?"

Don Quixote listened attentively. When the canon was done speaking he observed him in silence for some time. Finally he said, "If I'm not mistaken, sir, your comments were intended to convince me that there have never been knights errant; that books of chivalry are false, lying, harmful, and of no use to society; and that I have done wrong to read them, worse to believe them, and worst of all to follow in their footsteps. Furthermore, you deny the existence of Amadis of Gaul and all the other knights whose lives those books recount."

"That is precisely what I meant," the canon said.

"Well then," said Don Quixote, "in my opinion it is yourself who is deranged and under a spell. For to attempt to convince anyone that there were no such people as Amadis or the other knights would be like trying to persuade him that the sun doesn't shine nor the earth yield sustenance.

"Please, sir, give these books another chance. You'll be amazed at how they keep sadness at arm's length and are a tonic for the spirit. For myself, I can honestly say that since I became a knight errant I have been brave, courteous, generous, well-mannered, polite, bold, gentle, and patient; I've endured trials, travails, and spells; and even though at the moment I happen to be locked up in a madman's cage, I believe that, with God's grace, in a few days' time my own strong arm will make me ruler of some kingdom, where I shall be able to dispense the gratitude and generosity this heart of mine contains, especially toward Sancho Panza, my poor squire and the best man in the world. I wish I could grant him the countship I've long promised, but I fear he may be ill-suited to govern his estate."

Sancho, who had overheard these last few words, now joined the conversation. "I don't understand all this philosophy," he said. "What I do know is that the minute I become a count I'll know exactly what to do. My soul is as big as the next man's and my body as solid, and I'd be as much the king of my estate as any monarch. If I were king, I'd do exactly what I liked; and doing what I liked, I'd be delighted; and being delighted, I'd want nothing more; and wanting nothing more, there's nothing more to say—so bring on the kingdom and we'll see, as one blind man told the other."

"That's all well and good," the canon said, "but there is still a great deal more to be said on the matter of countships."

To which Don Quixote answered, "I don't know what else there is to say. I myself am guided by the example of the great Amadis of Gaul, who made his squire Count of the Firm Isle. That's all I need to make Sancho a count, for I count him one of the best squires who ever served a knight."

The canon was astonished by the well-reasoned nonsense that escaped Don Quixote's lips and by the way he had been taken in by the deliberate lies he had read in books. He marveled too at Sancho's foolishness in so ardently desiring the countship his master promised him.

They were roused from this discussion by a trumpet call so sad that they all turned to see whence it had come. "That solemn note," said Don Quixote, struggling to his feet, "is the summons to my next adventure."

What he saw when he looked out over the valley was a group of men dressed entirely in white coming down the side of a small hill.

The reason was this: that year the clouds had withheld their moisture from the earth, and now, from one end of the province to the other, processions, pilgrimages, and all manner of devotions were being held to persuade the Lord to open His forgiving hands and send down rain. To this end, the inhabitants of a nearby village were wending their way to a holy shrine that stood on a small rise just inside the valley.

For reasons known only to himself, Don Quixote forgot the many times in his life when he had seen religious penitents wearing equally strange clothes. He was convinced the men in white were the object of his next adventure, one to which he alone, as a knight errant, was being called. This interpretation was strengthened by the black-draped figure in their midst, a great lady, he imagined, whom these scurrilous thugs had abducted from her home. No sooner had this thought entered his mind than he sprang toward Rocinante, leapt onto his back, and asked Sancho Panza for his sword and shield. "Now, valiant friends, you shall know chivalry's true worth; for now, with your own eyes, you shall behold a captive lady instantly set free."

With this he dug his heels into Rocinante's sides and flew straight toward the penitents. Neither the priest, the canon, nor the barber could do anything to stop him, and even Sancho's shouts fell on deaf ears. "Where are you going, Don Quixote?" he cried. "Don't you see that you're about to attack a procession of religious penitents and that your captive lady is a statue of the Blessed Virgin?"

But his master was so intent on reaching the white-sheeted figures and freeing the lady in black that he didn't hear a word;

in any case, he would not have turned around even if the king himself had ordered him to do so.

"You with the covered faces," he called out in a hoarse and angry voice when he reached the procession. "Stop where you are and listen carefully to what I am about to say."

The first to stop were the men carrying the Virgin. "Speak quickly, brother," they replied, "for we cannot, indeed must not, interrupt what we are doing."

"I'll be brief," said Don Quixote. "In a word, you must immediately free your beautiful captive, for her tears and doleful face tell me you have borne her off against her will. I, who was born to right such wrongs, cannot stand idly by without making sure that she retrieves her long-lost liberty."

From this speech Don Quixote's listeners concluded that he was a madman and began to laugh. But their merriment only fueled the fire of his wrath. Without saying another word, he whipped out his sword and attacked the litter on which the holy image rode. One of the penitents quickly counterattacked with a forked stick, and before he knew it Don Quixote was spread-eagled on the ground.

In the meantime, the rest of Don Quixote's party came running up to where he lay. The frightened penitents lifted their hoods over their faces and began to dance around the image to protect it from attack. But fortune favored them beyond all expectation, for as soon as Sancho Panza caught sight of Don Quixote, he threw himself upon his master's body and began to raise the saddest, most ridiculous lament in the whole world, believing he was dead.

One of the priests in the procession recognized the curate, and with this the tempers of both groups began to cool. The curate gave the other priest a brief account of Don Quixote, and then they all went over to see if the wounded knight was really dead. It was there they overheard Sancho Panza's tearful words.

"O flower of chivalry, struck down by a single blow! O honor to your race, pride and glory of La Mancha and the world, which in your absence will be overrun by thieves and scoundrels! O knight generous beyond emperors and kings, who after I had served you only eight months offered me the brightest isle of the seas! Defier of dangers, enemy of lies, lover without cause! Imitator of the good, scourge to the bad—in short, knight errant, which says more than words can tell!"

Sancho's cries brought Don Quixote to. "He who lives without you, sweet Dulcinea," he said as soon as he opened his eyes, "knows even greater suffering than this. Help me onto my enchanted cart, Sancho, for I'm in no condition to ride Rocinante."

"I'd be delighted, Your Worship," Sancho said. "I propose that we return to our village with these gentlemen, whose only concern is for your welfare. From there we'll plan another journey, which with a little luck will bring us greater fame and fortune."

When Don Quixote agreed, the canon, the priest, and the barber congratulated him on his decision and, after savoring Sancho's comments to the full, helped him back up on the cart. The canon asked the priest to let him know how everything turned out, and here they parted company, with only the priest, the barber, Sancho Panza, and the faithful Rocinante, who was as patient as his master, remaining to accompany Don Quixote home. The wagoner hitched his oxen to the cart and the procession set off, traveling at the same leisurely pace as before.

After six days they arrived at Don Quixote's village. It was a Sunday afternoon, and the square was full of people. Everyone came running to see what was in the oxcart, and when they recognized their neighbor Don Quixote, their mouths fell open with amazement. A boy ran off to tell Don Quixote's housekeeper and niece that their long-lost master and uncle was back, lying yellow-faced and haggard on a pile of hay atop an oxcart. It was pitiful to hear the shouts the two women raised, and the curses they hurled anew against his books of chivalry, all of which they repeated when they saw Don Quixote come through the door.

At the news of Don Quixote's return, Sancho Panza's wife

came running, since she knew her husband had gone off to be his squire. As soon as she saw Sancho, she asked after his ass, to which Sancho replied that his ass had returned in better shape than his poor master.

"The Lord be praised," his wife replied. "But tell me, friend, what do you have to show for all your squiring? Have you brought me a fine dress or new shoes for our children?"

"I've brought nothing of the sort," said Sancho Panza, "but I have other things of even greater value and importance."

"Let me see," said his wife. "I need something to gladden my poor heart, which has been so sad and lonely all these months we were apart."

"Don't rush me, Juana Panza," Sancho said. "But I'll tell you one thing. There's nothing more beautiful in the whole world than for an honest man to squire a knight errant. Of course, out of every hundred adventures you embark on, ninety-nine don't work out the way you hoped. I've been blanket-tossed and I've been bruised; still, nothing can compare with waiting for the next adventure, crossing mountains, combing woods, climbing rocks, visiting castles, and staying in luxurious inns without paying a cent."

While Sancho Panza was talking to his wife, the housekeeper and niece helped Don Quixote off with his clothes and laid him in his ancient bed. He stared at them with wild eyes, completely oblivious to where he was. After recounting the lengths to which they had gone to bring him home, the priest urged the niece to lavish every possible attention on her uncle and keep a careful watch to prevent him from escaping. At this the two women began to wail afresh. Once more they cursed all books of chivalry and implored Heaven to consign the authors of such nonsense to the deepest pits of hell. They were afraid that the minute Don Quixote felt well enough they would once again find themselves alone. And they were right, for in the end everything turned out exactly as they had imagined.

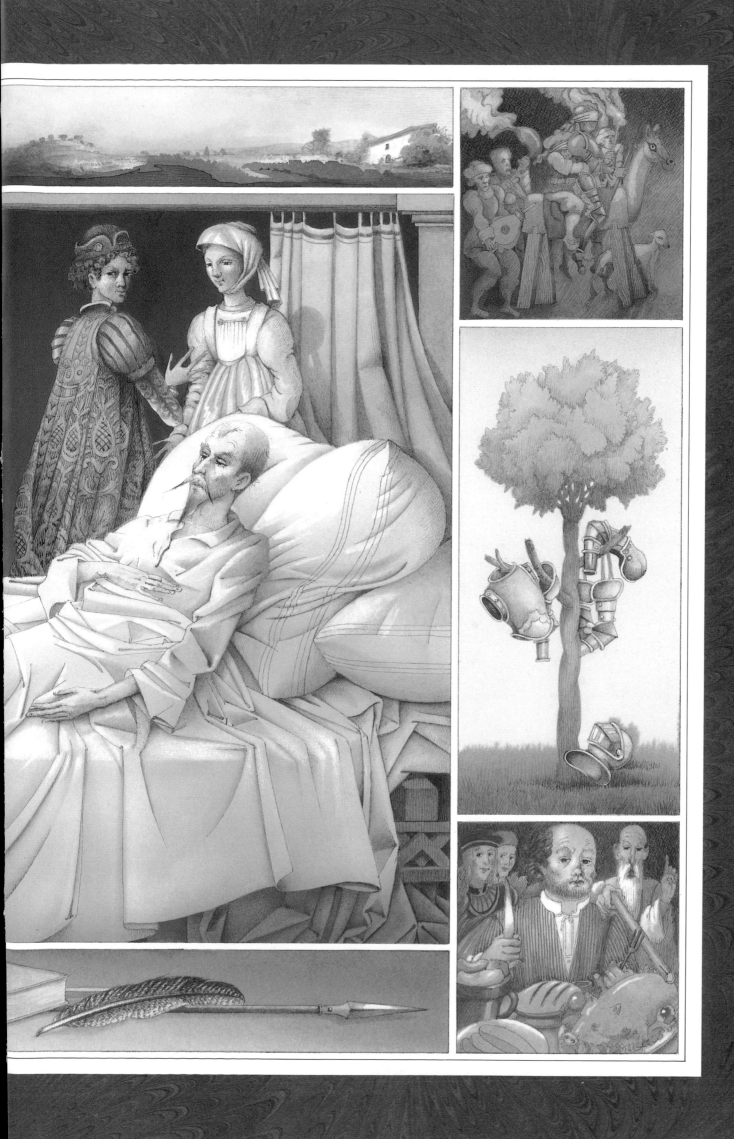

Design by Joel Avirom

Set in Packard Bold by
Printing Prep Inc., Buffalo, New York

Printed and bound by
Arnoldo Mondadori Editore, S.p.A., Verona, Italy